Tiny Tales

East Midlands

First published in Great Britain in 2007 by
Young Writers, Remus House, Coltsfoot Drive,
Peterborough, PE2 9JX
Tel (01733) 890066 Fax (01733) 313524
All Rights Reserved

Disclaimer
Young Writers has maintained every effort
to publish stories that will not cause offence.
Any stories, events or activities relating to individuals
should be read as fictional pieces and not construed
as real-life character portrayal.

Foreword

Young Writers was established in 1991, with the aim of encouraging the children and young adults of today to think and write creatively. Our latest primary school competition, *Tiny Tales*, posed an exciting challenge for these young authors: to write, in no more than fifty words, a story encompassing a beginning, a middle and an end. We call this the mini saga.

Tiny Tales East Midlands is our latest offering from the wealth of young talent that has mastered this incredibly challenging form. With such an abundance of imagination, humour and ability evident in such a wide variety of stories, these young writers cannot fail to enthral and excite with every tale.

Contents

Whitwick St John the Baptist CE Primary School, Coalville

The Mini Sagas

The One Penalty

This is it, the one penalty to win the football match, I was trembling with anxiety, the ball went flying and I scored. The noise of the crowd was amazing, people jumping up and down, I was crying with joy.
Then it all went silent, the PS2 game had crashed.

Brad Dalton (11)
Bellinge Primary School, Northampton

15

Petrified Molly

Suddenly she crept backwards, slowly *creek!* Her knees were knocking together. *Argh!* Molly was petrified. She was sure Matty told her to meet him in the old haunted mansion. She went to 80 doors, shut. 'I'm trapped!' She heard someone shout her name. She looked up, it's Matty all alone.

Natasha Avis (11)
Canon Peter Hall CE Primary School, Immingham

The Haunted House

As I walked through the door of the mansion, the grand staircase swept before me. I heard a monster coming up. I felt its breath. It started licking me. I noticed it was a tiger. Then I started to wake up and I noticed it was my dog licking me.

Luke Dwyer (10)
Canon Peter Hall CE Primary School, Immingham

17

Scary Mary

Mary was in the field playing with her frisbee.
Suddenly she threw it too hard and it went into
the pylon.
'Oh no, Mummy help, I need you.'
'Why?'
'Just come!'
'Why?'
'Because I said why.'
Bzzzzzzzzz, scary Mary!

Georgia Ayres (10)
Canon Peter Hall CE Primary School, Immingham

Alone, Too Alone

Jess was walking in the dark room, thinking she was alone. What was that? She heard something banging. *Bang, bang,* something was there. She walked to the door where the banging was coming from in the dark room. It was coming from the cupboard.
'Found you, your turn!'

Kassandra Dyer (10)
Canon Peter Hall CE Primary School, Immingham

The High Ladder

I stepped up the ladder. It was so high. I was really scared. As I went higher I got more scared. I didn't think I could make it. I got to the top and tied myself up. The man pushed me off!
It was only the zipline - what fun!

Robynne Brooks (11)
Canon Peter Hall CE Primary School, Immingham

Untitled

In the jungle the most dreaded beast - brown and tall, pointy, jagged teeth, flat nose. I could feel him breathing down my neck. I could hear him breathing. 'That was close, he almost got my leg!' He's growling at me. He's getting ready to pounce on me. It's my dog.

Myles Towler (11)
Canon Peter Hall CE Primary School, Immingham

The Scary Monster In The Closet

The closet door creaked, from head to toe I was shaking. As I moved closer I became even more scared. I could hear someone laughing. I shouted my mum, but she couldn't hear me. That's when I thought I would go in. I opened it and I saw … my sister!

Macauley Lane (11)
Canon Peter Hall CE Primary School, Immingham

Alien Hominid

FBI agents searched for the alien who had previously caused so much trouble.
'Where could he be?' questioned a rookie agent.
Suddenly the armoured car's lights turned black so did the street lights. Luminous teeth marks appeared on the bonnet of a car.
Footsteps were heard behind them … silence.

Luke Tetley (10)
Canon Peter Hall CE Primary School, Immingham

The Coaster

We went up further, higher, then we stopped. A sudden drop, screams came from every corner. A ghost tried to scare me and it worked! Wolves howling, werewolves growling, we stopped again then flew round the corner. I got off. I will never go on a ghost ride ever again.

Jessie Palmer (10)
Canon Peter Hall CE Primary School, Immingham

Tricky Tigers

Something wanders around, *crackle, crack, creak*. Sticks crunching and a draught of wind blows down Kelly's back. Something roars. Kelly jumps out of her skin. She turns round with a big breeze whooshing past her. 'Get off the PlayStation!' Kelly shouts as her little brother rushes past her.

Kayleigh Gregory (10)
Canon Peter Hall CE Primary School, Immingham

The Monster

I felt a gush of water on my back. I turned around. There in front of me was a monster. It came up to me and opened its jaw … and licked me. It was my dog Fred. Boy he does look scary underwater.

Lydia Urquhart-Smith (11)
Canon Peter Hall CE Primary School, Immingham

The Scary Ride

The ride was tall. I kept looking at it, how scary it was. I walked up to it, slowly looking down, thinking I had to have a go so I got on it. It started going up and down fast. I felt sick but excited, I wanted to get off!

Courtney Warne (9)
Canon Peter Hall CE Primary School, Immingham

Untitled

All I could hear was the keys in the door rattling.
It scared me. Just then I heard someone come
in the door. I shouted, 'Who is there?'
'It is only me, your dad.'
'You scared me, I thought you were a burglar,
does Mum know you are here?'

Naomi Groves (9)
Canon Peter Hall CE Primary School, Immingham

How Exciting

Can't sleep, so excited, I fly for the first time
tomorrow.
The airport is full of people dashing around.
At last I see the aeroplane. Now I feel sick and
scared. It's OK Dad will hold my hand. The
engines roar, the wheels turn and up we go.
How exciting.

Jasmyne Knights (9)
Canon Peter Hall CE Primary School, Immingham

Monster Under The Covers

Frizzy hair stuck out everywhere, bulging bloodshot eyes that glared menacingly. It had a wonky nose. Its chin jutted out, as if it was the craggy face of the mountains. Its teeth were as yellow as the sun and he muttered big groans. Dad had just got out of bed.

Mackenzie Cuthbert (9)
Canon Peter Hall CE Primary School, Immingham

A New Nose

Poof - suddenly there was green smoke everywhere. It should have been blue. Oh no, what had I done wrong this time? It was meant to give me a nice pretty nose, only now it was big and hairy! How can I put it right again? 'Someone help me please!'

Bethany Hotchin (9)
Canon Peter Hall CE Primary School, Immingham

31

Monster Attack

Ben walked down his street. He heard a crash
and bang. He was very nervous, he wanted
to see what happened. Before he could, a
monster popped out of nowhere. He was very,
very scared, he could not move, he started to
scream and ran as fast as lightning.

Ben Patterson (9)
Canon Peter Hall CE Primary School, Immingham

Strange Noises

All I could hear was the jangle of keys in the door and it slamming too. I jumped nervously at every noise. I pulled the brown heavy door towards me. I looked around and saw two rows of people staring at me. I went back inside and read my book.

Jodie Blades (9)
Canon Peter Hall CE Primary School, Immingham

Dinosaurs

My hands trembled, my muscles were all tight.
I heard a noise, a terrifying noise. What was
it? Where was it coming from? It was coming
closer, closer, the ground was shaking. I looked
to the right, I looked to the left, I saw nothing.
It's huge,
I hate dinosaurs.

Emma Tulloch (9)
Canon Peter Hall CE Primary School, Immingham

34

A Day In The Life Of An Alien

Where is my mum? I am in a strange room. A lady is putting me on a table, she's wearing a white coat. I start to feel sleepy, my eyes begin to close. I try to keep them open. She's putting something on me but I can't get it off.

Caitlin Horton (9)
Canon Peter Hall CE Primary School, Immingham

The Seaside Adventure

Mum said, 'We're going to the beach.' I got my bucket and spade.
When we got to the beach, I swam in the sea.
After a while, a big sandman jumped out of the sand.
'It's trying to eat me!' shouted Emma, then Superman rescued her. They had a celebration.

Abbe Urquhart-Smith (8)
Canon Peter Hall CE Primary School, Immingham

The Nightmare

There was a boy and his bed was about to eat him up. It was sucking up everything into its mouth and the boy was slipping. Just as it was about to eat him, his mum called him to breakfast.

Phew! Safe now, thought the boy.

Matthew Arthur (8)
Canon Peter Hall CE Primary School, Immingham

The Alien

One day, in a little town called Neptune, two little boys, Levi and Luke, were messing in the town centre. Then before you knew it, Levi got lost. Then Levi thought he saw an alien in a field. He ran away, not knowing it was Luke. Or was it?

Andrew Brooks (10)
Canon Peter Hall CE Primary School, Immingham

New York City Danger

Last week something amazing happened. No
I didn't finish school. An evil scientist came to
New York City to rule it. He made a hypnotising
machine, to hypnotise the citizens of New York.
After a day, everyone was hypnotised, apart
from Joshua and Levi, the superheroes.

Joshua Parker (10)
Canon Peter Hall CE Primary School, Immingham

39

Crystal

As I saw the sparkles coming out of the ground, Laura, Ciara and I stood there in amazement. Laura pulled the crystal out of the ground. Suddenly Laura went into the tent next door and then went back but when she got back, the floor collapsed underneath her. She left …

Rebekah Parkin (10)
Canon Peter Hall CE Primary School, Immingham

Untitled

One day there was a girl called Lauren. Just then she heard a funny noise so she went downstairs to see what it was.

'Oh never mind, it was just a hedgehog,' said Lauren and she went back up the stairs to her big comfy large and cuddly bed.

Lauren Raithby (9)
Canon Peter Hall CE Primary School, Immingham

Mary Had A Little Lamb

Mary was a little lamb, it was very funny. It always bounced up and down and it also ran around the field.
When the farmer's sheepdog comes out, the farmer blows a whistle that only the sheepdog can hear and makes little Mary's lamb go in the pen.

Abbey Bedford (8)
Canon Peter Hall CE Primary School, Immingham

The Fantastic Four

On Saturday Fantastic Four and his brother went into the woods. Fantastic Four made his brother jump and all of his veins popped out of his head.

'Quick, quick go home!'

By the time they got home Fantastic Four died so his brother rang an ambulance.

Nicole Louise Fleming (8)
Canon Peter Hall CE Primary School, Immingham

The Sea Monster

They sailed across the treacherous sea when all of a sudden, a sea monster rumbled the sea with its roar. The Vikings set the cannons to fire at the sea monster. The sea monster got angry and then it went away with a growl.

Gary Williams (8)
Canon Peter Hall CE Primary School, Immingham

Untitled

Jack landed in Dangerland, he saw a huge green goblin. He trembled in his socks. The goblin was four times the size of him. He was shaking like he was going to fall off a ladder. The goblin moved his head, blinked and yawned. Jack ran for it.

Chloe Orchard (8)
Canon Peter Hall CE Primary School, Immingham

A Naughty Little Fairy

There was once a fairy called Daisy. She had long blondey-browny hair. She was in trouble. She had to go to her mum and tell her that she had been naughty at school. She wasn't allowed out for another week. She was dead upset and very bored!

Brittany Wardle (11)
Coppice Primary School, Heanor

Larry Trotter's Big Adventure

Larry Trotter and Con Squeezly stood in the dungeon, their wands outstretched, waiting for Larry's enemy (he who must be tamed), Lord Stalumart. Lermine Manger came running into the dungeon screaming. All of a sudden, the door blasted open. Out came a beaming light, Headstick, Larry's owl, flew out.

William Hufton (11)
Coppice Primary School, Heanor

Aeroplane!

Tim was going on holiday to Greece. He boarded the 747. It took off. Then the 747 went into a downfall headIng for Athens. *Boom!* It hit the floor and then skidded down the runway and then stopped at the end of the runway. What a landing.

Louis Abbott (11)
Coppice Primary School, Heanor

Tabby And Godmother

Tabby hated her spoilt stepsister. One day
Tabby was sweeping up, when a fairy appeared
and explained she was Tabby's godmother.
Tabby told her that she wanted to go to a ball.
Whoosh, suddenly Tabby was in a beautiful
room. She danced with the prince.
Six months later, they married.

Molly Attenborough (11)
Coppice Primary School, Heanor

The Loch Ness Monster

Thomas was walking past Loch Ness when suddenly the ground trembled. A green head poked out of the water and Thomas screamed, 'It's the Loch Ness monster!' Thomas ran away. 'Why does everyone run away from me?' cried the green head. 'I was only being friendly.' Thomas never went back.

Jake Campbell (11)
Coppice Primary School, Heanor

Survival Series

Tom's in an aeroplane, he's going to Croatia.
The plane's lost its wing. Then the plane
tears apart and then suddenly, all of them are
screaming, heading for the jungle.
'What's that - a 747? We're going to die.'
They have parachutes. This isn't the end of the
jungle for Tom.

Phillip Marriott (11)
Coppice Primary School, Heanor

Simpsons

Ding ... ding ... The school bell, he ran
to school just in time. He was late, he got
detention. He had to write *never be late* 50
times.
When he got home, he played with Jake, then
played tricks on Sophie, his sister.

Nadine Smith (10)
Coppice Primary School, Heanor

Birthday Treat

It was my eleventh birthday and my mum was
making me a cake.
'Ben can you get some eggs from the pantry?'
said my mum.
'OK,' I replied.
I ran down into the pantry only to find my
friends. 'Surprise!' they shouted.

Ben Saxton (11)
Coppice Primary School, Heanor

The Present

It was nearly Christmas, just 24 hours to go. Chris was woken by a rustling noise. He looked at the bottom of the Christmas tree. He picked up a present that was wiggling about, opened it and saw it was a robot programmed to do horrible things. Chris woke up.

Jake Pulford (11)
Coppice Primary School, Heanor

Shrek's Epic Quest

Snap! went the twig as Shrek stumbled through the forest. 'Hurry up Donkey we have to get Arthur before midnight.'
'I'm going as fast as I can and my feet are killing me!'
Just then Shrek arrived in a mysterious place …

Jonathan Krakowiak (11)
Coppice Primary School, Heanor

Snowy And The Banana

Snowy had an evil stepmother. She ran away from home and lived with twelve kind men. She looked after them very well. Her stepmother cast a spell on her, using a banana to make her sleepy. A prince found her and woke her and they lived together.

Beverley Jarvis (11)
Coppice Primary School, Heanor

56

The Destroyer

Jeffery walked down the narrow path in the woods. Suddenly he heard a yelp! He started to feel woozy. He then turned around and saw a big blue bulky alien with big green eyes! He didn't know what to do … Then the alien grabbed him, destroyed him and he flew home.

Conner Young (11)
Coppice Primary School, Heanor

The UFO

One day a boy named Corie was riding on his bike down the street. Suddenly a UFO flew over his head. 'Wow!' said Corie.
The UFO landed on the floor. Corie hid behind a bin to see what would happen but the UFO just flew away and Corie went home.

Kane Flinders (11)
Coppice Primary School, Heanor

Home Alone

I knew I wasn't alone. Why didn't I go with Mum? A shiver through, told me all I wanted to know. I switched the telly on to give me company. A rumble from outside, I ran to the door. A flash of light, my mum was back.

Grace Clark (11)
Gretton Primary School, Corby

Untitled

I walked upstairs, it was dark, the stairs creaked. I shouted, 'Mum!' No answer so I started to run back down. Then I just switched the light. Then I heard a high-pitched noise, then a car noise. Oh it was Jack. Then Mum jumped out and shouted, 'Boo!'

Charlie Irwin (10)
Gretton Primary School, Corby

Zombie

I was running around the street trying to avoid being bitten by the zombies. One of them grabbed my arm. I tried to wiggle free but there's no escape. It bites my arm, I got free and ran to my house and locked the door. I turned into a zombie.

Jake Villette (10)
Gretton Primary School, Corby

The Killer Mars Bar

It's out there, somewhere in the woods, lurking among the trees. I can hear it as it moves in the bushes. Look east, no look west. Quick we have to save it. It's an endangered species. Don't let that guy eat it. That's a killer Mars bar.

Melissa Dolby (11)
Gretton Primary School, Corby

Shark Attack

I dived into the water, it was dark and it got even darker. The sea was black and then I saw a huge tail, then a massive fin. The mouth opened and it bit me, right through the heart and tons of blood spilt everywhere.

Sam Stocks (11)
Gretton Primary School, Corby

Flying Up High

As I stepped into the tunnel, I drifted up and
up, spit dripped from my mouth and the air
pressed against my whole body. Soon I thought
I was actually flying and suddenly I was floating
down. The instructor took hold of me and we
floated up towards the top.

Sophie Ferguson (11)
Gretton Primary School, Corby

Who Is It?

Step, step, step, someone's in the house, who is it? Jim is in his room, doing his extremely boring maths homework. He slowly crept down his really creaky stairs. 'Hello?' Jim whispered. 'Hello?' Jim whispered a bit louder. Suddenly, *'Boo*, I'm coming to suck your blood.'
It's a vampire, *argh!*

Matthew Wymant (10)
Gretton Primary School, Corby

The Whirling Wind

'Wheee,' this is fun! I'm whizzing round a freezing cold room. All I can hear is my heart beating. The window is open and the wind is screaming in my ears. The door opens, 'Hi Mum.'
I cringe, the screaming is her. 'Tidy your room. Stop bouncing on your bed!'

Lori Hodson (10)
Gretton Primary School, Corby

My Dog

My mum walked into the room. She was carrying a box with holes in the side. She said it was for me. I approached it not knowing what to expect. I opened the box, a beagle puppy jumped out. She was white, tan and cute all over.

Molly Haley (10)
Gretton Primary School, Corby

Being Followed

The leaves crackled as she ran through the woods, hoping that it wouldn't catch up with her. She could feel her legs getting weak and the footsteps getting closer.
Suddenly the footsteps that had been scurrying behind her had stopped. She felt a big heavy hand grab her shoulder …

Hayley Newcombe (11)
Henry Whipple Junior School, Nottingham

The Unexpected

I was scared. The thing was coming right at me.
I didn't know what to do, it was ugly and green.
It had yellow teeth.
'Hello,' it said in a strange voice.
Oddly, I knew that voice, it smelt of cheese.
It turned out to be my sister. How weird.

Katherine Carter (11)
Henry Whipple Junior School, Nottingham

The Thing!

It was stood there looking at me, moaning and groaning, it flinched … Suddenly I was being chased by a thing! The huge footsteps racing towards me. My heart thumping out of my footsteps. I wanted to go home. Seeing my mum in my head made me feel even more scared.

Rebecca Johnson (11)
Henry Whipple Junior School, Nottingham

The Magic Sea

I'm slowly moving forwards in a wonderful sea.
There are many coloured flowers and fish!
However, it's very quiet but I'm breaking it up
by the sound of my breathing. The lovely fish
swim behind dirty rocks. The sea was still and
calm. I felt I was being watched.

Jack Walters (11)
Henry Whipple Junior School, Nottingham

Shadows

I lay my head back and closed my eyes. I heard *bang!* I opened my eyes, a shadow crept around the corner. My heart was pounding, sweat trickled down my back. My thumping head was about to explode That's the last time I lend my witch costume to my dad.

Emma Sims (11)
Kensington Junior School, Ilkeston

Down!

My heart pounding getting closer and closer, twisting, winding, going round. I shut my eyes, sweat crept down my back. I tightly clutched onto the bar screaming. My hair waving in the wind. Then suddenly, 'Argh!' with myself back on the ground. Let's go on the flume again.

Charlotte Purnell (11)
Kensington Junior School, Ilkeston

Snap!

My heart was racing, my hands were sticky and clammy. I looked down, the trampoline was no longer beneath me and the ground grew ever closer as I came hurtling towards Earth at the speed of light.
Snap! I'm in the bush aren't I?

Emily Bower (11)
Kensington Junior School, Ilkeston

Untitled

I walk into the room, sweat running down my
back. I begin to climb the steps, although my
fingers are numb. Eyes staring from below.
I slither along, I slip. *Argh!* I land safely,
water flowing through my nose. I hear an …
applause. I made it through the daring dive.

Autumn Hill (11)
Kensington Junior School, Ilkeston

Something Isn't Right

I glance in the mirror waiting for my whole
new look, just hiding behind my old towel.
Something doesn't feel quite right. I take away
the towel, the mirror cracks. My jaw drops … oh
no, my hair is green.

Emma Frost (11)
Kensington Junior School, Ilkeston

Can't Leave

I feel weird and alone. My face feels cold and empty, my hands are trembling. I step outside, I look in a car mirror and run back inside, upstairs and into my bedroom and lock the door.
Man I need my make-up today.

Sophie Rice (11)
Kensington Junior School, Ilkeston

On The Edge

I was on the edge, my hand shivered, the lights blinded me. The damp floor sticking to my feet. I became all sweaty inside. I took a deep breath, I jumped and fell.
'I'm falling!' The shouting came towards me. A splash! I knew that swimming was not my thing.

Bethany Guilford (11)
Kensington Junior School, Ilkeston

Eeww!

My eyes were stinging as the powerful aroma surrounded me. My nostrils were aflame with the foul stench. My throat started to close. I felt sick, there was a loud crack as I hurtled the bottle across the town. I knew I shouldn't have bought that cheap perfume.

Rosie Spence (11)
Kensington Junior School, Ilkeston

Ouch!

We were thrashing about in all directions, skidding and crashing into everything in sight. Suddenly we saw a man in front of us. We tried to stop but we're too late. His foot was squashed.
Aren't I a good dodgem driver?

Lucy Bentley (11)
Kensington Junior School, Ilkeston

My Parents Are Aliens

Ella loved her parents. She came home from school and her parents were gone. She thought they had gone to the shop so she turned the news on when two aliens came on the telly. Lisa and John Moonlight, Ella's parents, had turned into aliens.

Oh no - what happened?

Shannon Beer (10)
Kensington Junior School, Ilkeston

Ouch!

My hand plunged forward, I reached for it. The
smell in front gassed me. Oh no! It's moved
again. My fingers trembling. Hooray, I've caught
it! Giving out a shriek. *Argh!*
I wish I didn't have to clean out the hamster.

Anna Tobutt (11)
Kensington Junior School, Ilkeston

Up And Down

My heart pounded. My stomach rose as I went up. I came towards the ground. I started sweating, my face turned purple. Up, down, I felt sick. I flung from wall to wall. As I flew I left my belly in one place, me in another … I hate bouncy castles.

Freya Smyth Callard (11)
Kensington Junior School, Ilkeston

It's Getting Hot In Here

Sweat was dribbling down my spine. My cheeks were puffing with redness. My blood was burning my skin. I couldn't take it any longer. I felt like I was going to burst. I thought I was going to pass out. It was horrible.
'Are you finished yet in the sauna?'

Hayley Mills (11)
Kensington Junior School, Ilkeston

Jumping

With a flick of the wrist it roared to life. The lights flashed, the fire burnt, it sped forward up the ramp. It flew like a rocket, as my flab wobbled I felt my dinner. I landed safely on my bike. That was the best jump I had done.

Sam Briggs (11)
Kensington Junior School, Ilkeston

85

The Cream Clouds

I'm floating through the blue blanket on a delicious dollop of ice cream whilst birds fly by and say hello.
The ice cream began to melt. Oh no! What was I to do? There was no way I'd survive. I really shouldn't have eaten cheese last night.

Georgina Rudd (11)
Kensington Junior School, Ilkeston

Home Alone

The boy looked out of his telescope. He saw robbers! They were looking for a chip. The boy had it but he didn't know that yet. They didn't have masks on. They had police gloves on so they didn't leave fingerprints on the things, but they didn't find the chip.

Niall Hardaker (10)
Killisick Junior School, Nottingham

Little Red Riding Hood

She dramatically skipped through the dark night. All of a sudden a huge angry wolf jumped out of a big tree. He quickly pushed her over so he could get to the place where she was going first. He wanted to eat her up but the woodchopper saved her.

Megan Swift (10)
Killisick Junior School, Nottingham

Rodney And The Haunted House

Rodney crept up to the door of the house. He opened the door and crept up the stairs. The door slammed shut! He looked around shaking. He ran downstairs, tried to open the door but it was locked. He was trapped! The light flickered, 'Get out of bed Rodney.'

Liam Cunningham (9)
Killisick Junior School, Nottingham

The Hairdresser

A girl skipped into the hairdressers. She sat down and looked in the mirror, it wasn't her reflection. 'Trim please.'
The hairdresser didn't give her a trim, she cut half her hair off.
'Oh no, that's not what I asked for.'
'You asked for that, you look funny.'

Megan Ingle (10)
Killisick Junior School, Nottingham

Untitled

I was alone. A light as big as the moon covered the window. I couldn't see, there was a knocking at the door.
Bang! I was too scared to answer it. Weird noises were coming from outside.
'Let me in.'
A key went in the door, it was my mum.

Phoenix Michell (10)
Killisick Junior School, Nottingham

The Spooky House

Aargh! Lightning struck.
'Where am I? Go away, who are you?' cried
Megan,
'Nooo, it's me,' cried the zombie.
It looked like Lauren, Megan wished it was her
friend Lauren. Megan was panicking, sweat
dripped down her back. 'Don't hurt me,' cried
Megan,
'Wake up, school time,' shouted Megan's
mother.

Kassie Newby (10)
Killisick Junior School, Nottingham

92

The Beast And The Sun

A gigantic beast went charging at a building.
Crash! 'That thing's killed my sister.'
Emma ran to Demeter to explain, 'You're the
only person who can help.'
Demeter had an idea. She flew to the blazing,
orange sun. She peeled an enormous bit off the
sun. *Drop!* The beast crumpled.

Lauren Stredder (9)
Killisick Junior School, Nottingham

The Big Shed

I saw a shed in the distance. I ran to see if anybody was in there. I knocked on the door and rang the crooked big doorbell. No one answered. I went inside and found a treasure chest, but nothing was in there.

Emerson Whitham (8)
Killisick Junior School, Nottingham

What Is That?

Nicola, Megan and Kaylee walked into the
woods.
'What's that?' muttered Megan.
'It's nothing,' yelled Nicola.
'Let's go in,' screamed Kaylee.
'No thanks, I'll wait out here!'
'Are you sure?'
'Yes, I'm going home.'
'Me too,' said Kaylee.
'Wait for me,' yelled Nicola.
'What was that?'
'I don't know.'

Kaylee Newby (8)
Killisick Junior School, Nottingham

Untitled

Jack and Lucy were lost in the woods. As they crept on to the slimy path Jack saw an old shop.
'Jack are you going to go in there?'
'Yes, are you?'
'No.'
As they opened the damp door, a voice screamed, 'Jack run.'
The children ran.

Jack Duffin (9)
Killisick Junior School, Nottingham

96

Untitled

The boys and I were walking down to the dark forest. There was a lion statue. I looked at it and I found a tiny door and some biscuits. We all ate one and became small. I screamed. We went through the door.
'Happy birthday Jake, everyone is here.'

Amrit Samra (9)
Killisick Junior School, Nottingham

The Nasty House

Matt and Lewis went to a nasty house and looked in there. There was a little teddy in the house.
'Let's go and see!'
Suddenly, a nasty thing came past. They fell in a dark hole.
'Who put us in this hole?'
Finally they went back to their home.

Michael Gee (7)
Killisick Junior School, Nottingham

The Mystery Light

Six years ago there were two brothers called Callum and Jack. They always played in the park where there was a mansion. Callum and Jack went in. They explored, they saw a burning light. Callum and Jack walked towards it and then no one ever saw them again.

Callum Powis (8)
Killisick Junior School, Nottingham

The Spooky Shed

The children walked closer to the shed, then went in. The door slammed shut. There was no escape! They looked through the window and saw a shadow move across. The children grabbed each other in fear of what could happen next. The spooky noise was heard again.

'Now what?'

Nicola Caines (9)
Killisick Junior School, Nottingham

Nightfall

2.45pm - Matt and Steven ran home. Suddenly
it turned pure darkness.
'What's happening?' asked Matt.
A tornado started. It was heading straight
towards them.
'What are we going to do?' said Steven.
The tornado went straight through them, in half
or so they thought.
'It's a miracle,' shouted Steven.

Sam Jackson (9)
Killisick Junior School, Nottingham

The Mystery Of Them All

Sara and Rose skidded down the narrow path leading to the house near the graveyard. They slowly opened the door and a hall surrounded them with hundreds of spiders' webs. They looked around.

'Argh!'

Then they rushed out as fast as they could but there was no one at home.

Hannah Simmons (8)
Killisick Junior School, Nottingham

102

House Of Doom

Amber and Summa were going for a walk.
'Let's go in that house,' whispered Amber.
'No! We will get into trouble,' replied Summa.
'I'm going to eat you,' shrieked a voice.
'Come here my precious,' said the voice.
'Don't you dare do it,' yelled Mum.
'Join the party!' said Nic.

Chelsea Jamson (9)
Killisick Junior School, Nottingham

The Haunted Castle

Two girls were very brainy and clever. The girls went walking one day. There right in front of them was a large castle. The girls walked inside and walked into a monster. They skidded along the slippery floor. They ran and found a trapdoor. They slid down it and ran.

Holly Stevenson (8)
Killisick Junior School, Nottingham

The Haunted Mansion

The night was flowing. The days went on. Liam, Amrit, Jake and Sharif all went for a walk. They looked at a big scary mansion. A light flashed on! The mates looked at a big head poking out of the window. Then Jake and Amrit ran to the door and vanished.

Liam Redfearn (9)
Killisick Junior School, Nottingham

The Bad Day

'Mum, can I go to the dream room?'
'Yes,' replied Mum.
They went up to the haunted house and they didn't get caught.
'Tammie?' yelled Elane. There was no answer. Elane went upstairs and looked in the dream room. She thought they were out, but they had disappeared.

Paige Jamson (9)
Killisick Junior School, Nottingham

106

Untitled

Tammie was protecting Sophie, Sophie was frightened. They were starving as they had nothing to eat in days.

'This house looks haunted,' whispered Sophie.

'That's because it is.'

'Oh,' answered Sophie.

'C'mon, let's go inside and have a look.'

'OK.' I rang the doorbell and then I ran away.

Lara Powis (8)
Killisick Junior School, Nottingham

The Deep Dark Woods

They were going through the deep dark woods. All the trees came alive and they started to walk towards them. They ran but they couldn't find the way out. There was a shed, the girls went in and were safe. They fell asleep and later went home.

Megan Stacey (9)
Killisick Junior School, Nottingham

The Mysterious Shed

It was a cold winter's night, Jason and his puppy Sparky were walking in the forest. As they neared the shed Sparky started barking at a large banner that was blowing in the wind. Jason opened the rusty door.
'Surprise,' yelled his family.
'Wow, what a great party!' shouted Jason.

Tonisha Teale (9)
Killisick Junior School, Nottingham

The Headless Horse

Late at night Dr and Martha were driving in their car. Just then a headless horse ran in front of them.
'We must stop him!' shouted Dr.
They jumped out of the car and grabbed the horse. Then Dr used his sonic screwdriver and sent him back to Gouifray.

Daisy Donaghy (8)
Killisick Junior School, Nottingham

Scary Wood

One night Paige and Rachael went to the woods. They saw a big tree. Suddenly it moved. They were very scared. Paige and Rachael ran as fast as they could. The trees were running after them then they disappeared, it was quiet. They ran home and told Mum.

Rachael Perkins (9)
Killisick Junior School, Nottingham

111

Spooky Woods

I went to the woods with Rachael. Mum had said don't go in the woods. We saw a big tree that ran after us. I got scared, Rachael laughed because I fell over. I was upset. Mum found us, told us off and took us home for a hot drink.

Paige Longstaff (8)
Killisick Junior School, Nottingham

Spooky Woods

One night Emily took her dog for a walk in the dark woods. Suddenly she spotted a flash of white. She was terrified. She wanted to turn around and run. Just then, it moved again. She looked closely, it was only an old white T-shirt stuck in a large tree.

Abbie Webb (8)
Killisick Junior School, Nottingham

113

The Weird Day

One sunny morning Holly and Cerys were walking about in the street. They noticed there was no one else out and about.
'Why is there nobody about?' asked Holly.
'I don't know,' replied Cerys.
Everything was so weird so Holly and Cerys looked everywhere and there was nobody anywhere.
Weird.

Holly Knaggs (7)
Killisick Junior School, Nottingham

The Greedy Goat!

One sunny afternoon, Ben went to feed the
goats. There was a big problem. Nibbles, a
goat, was eating all the other goats' food.
'Stop that Nibbles,' Ben yelled.
'Baa baa baa,' Nibbles baaed back.
That's not fair, I thought to myself.
'I'll separate you, here you go,' I sighed.

Lauren Pengelly (8)
Killisick Junior School, Nottingham

The Haunted House

I stopped motionless as a big white hand
grabbed me.
'Where you taking me?' No one answered.
'Help, help, get me out of here.'
Suddenly it dropped me.
'Wake up,' called Mum. 'You are having a bad
dream.'

Mica Zacharski (7)
Killisick Junior School, Nottingham

Tiny Tales East Midlands

The Haunted House

One terrifying night two boys named Tim and Billy crept out of their bedroom. They ran to another house to see what was in it because it seemed haunted. Tim and Billy went through the back door of the haunted house. Tim was terrified. *'Argh!'* he shouted, 'there's a ...'

Imogen Sutherland (8)
Killisick Junior School, Nottingham

A Big Bang

The girls were playing and talking in the garden
when they suddenly heard a big bang. It was
coming from the house.
'What shall we do?'
'Where's Mum?'
Bang! There it was again. *Bang!* 'What shall we
do?'
They woke up and heard Mum.
'Mum.'
'Hello.'

Chelsie Gash (9)
Killisick Junior School, Nottingham

The Green Monster

I saw it! It opened its green slimy mouth and walked menacingly towards the cat crouching in the corner. A cold chill ran down my spine.
'Argh!' I heard myself scream.
The monster spun around.
Suddenly he turned into my eighteen-year-old son.

Gerard Milano (9)
Killisick Junior School, Nottingham

Spooky Woods

Joe and Chloe went to the woods and they got lost. There was thunder and lightning and Mum found them. Then they went home and had some tea and biscuits.

Andrea Subden (9)
Killisick Junior School, Nottingham

The White Man

The white man started to chase them. Suddenly
they couldn't find the man, he was hiding. He
was on top of the climbing frame.
'Help,' they shouted.
He laughed. 'I'm only from the circus.'
They both sighed with relief.

Amy Scotcher (8)
Killisick Junior School, Nottingham

121

The Haunted War

It was 1945, just me in my army troop survived. I was scared. The German army was coming at me. Suddenly I saw some of the corpses rising, bodies were plodding towards me. They were all around me … but they were defending me. I managed to escape and we won.

James Ahmet (8)
Killisick Junior School, Nottingham

The Ghost House

It was midnight and it was pitch-black. *Bang*
the front door slammed shut, then opened.
Bang, bang, bang, creak at the top of the stairs.
Footsteps.
'I am going to kill you,' a voice suddenly
whispered.
I fainted flat on the floor. The ghost went, I woke
up.

Kasey Wall (9)
Killisick Junior School, Nottingham

Scary Shock

My friends had dared me to come to this house.
Everyone said it's haunted. I didn't believe them
… until now! I heard footsteps above! With my
heart beating fast, I crept upstairs to the attic.
Slowly I opened the door. I gasped.
'It's disco time,' laughed my friends.
We boogied.

Kirsty Howland (9)
Killisick Junior School, Nottingham

The Haunted Mansion

I walked up the path. The house seemed
normal enough but when I went in lightning
crashed down. I saw figures in a shadowy
place.
'Why they following me?'
I ran into a room, I felt something close.
'Don't be silly Eric,' shouted Dad.
'Oh you're the scary figure.'

Eric Lee (9)
Killisick Junior School, Nottingham

Hallowe'en Mystery

Lightning hit the rooftops and rain lashed down on the long driveway. I needed shelter quickly, so I stumbled into the deserted house. Suddenly I heard a creak, then again, but louder and closer so I shouted, 'Anybody home?'

A door flung open.

'Happy Hallowe'en,' screamed my friends.

Benjamin Hyland (9)
Killisick Junior School, Nottingham

The Ghost House

'I bet you daren't go inside the house?' said my
friends.
'I do,' I said.
I ran in. I saw lots of funny looking shadows
creeping along. They screamed and shouted. I
was scared for the very first time. I saw a ghost
but then I saw my friends.

Matthew Parker (9)
Killisick Junior School, Nottingham

The Horrid House

I was walking down the street to my house
when I saw a figure walk in the haunted house.
Wondering, I crept after it. When I went in the
house, silence started to break, lightning and
thunder. I heard a sudden creak. The walls and
roof fell, unluckily on me!

Tim Cooper (8)
Killisick Junior School, Nottingham

Mysterious House

At the end of our street is a dark deserted house. One night Oliver dared us to go into the mysterious building. We opened the rotten door, *creak, bang*. A black figure shot across the room and blew dust everywhere. We pegged it home and never went back, ever again.

Daniel Swift (9)
Killisick Junior School, Nottingham

The Horrifying Movie

It was thundering. We'd no choice but to go in
the haunted cinema.
'That's got to be our death,' sobbed Daniel.
I replied, 'There is no choice.'
We entered the building then a weird figure
jumped out and Daniel fainted.
I picked him up and ran for my life.

Oliver Clay (9)
Killisick Junior School, Nottingham

The Collapsing Pyramid

I entered the dusty pyramid and disappeared into the darkness. I felt a shudder under my tiny feet then suddenly the steps moved, the walls cracked opened and the way out collapsed. Just then a mummy appeared.
'Was it Tutankhamen?' I yelled loudly, then …
'Wake up, you're late for school.'

Adam Hyland (9)
Killisick Junior School, Nottingham

The Freaky Shopping Centre

I walked further into the shopping centre. Suddenly I heard a noise. It was the door shutting. I ran towards it but … too late! I turned around and saw a beautiful mannequin. I went to touch it. Suddenly it came to life. It chased me. I ran for my life.

Georgia Bell (9)
Killisick Junior School, Nottingham

The Mysterious House

I was walking slowly to the house with a broken window and creepy doors. As I entered, I heard a scary noise. It came from upstairs, so I went up there. Suddenly I saw a shadow, the shadow was floating on the wall. I quickly ran out of the house.

Charlie Wilding (8)
Killisick Junior School, Nottingham

Jemma And Her Breakfast

Pop, crackle, pop, Jemma came in. She could hear it again. *Pop, crackle, pop,* she did not know what to do. She had a look upstairs. She could hear it still. She was frightened and then her mum came back from shopping.
'Oh Jemma you haven't eaten your breakfast yet.'

Sharif Walker (10)
Killisick Junior School, Nottingham

Charmed One

Dark Glider, he shot his arrow. It propelled into
Phebi's stomach. One of the charmed ones
was down. He fired another 'Energy', a ball of
colour. Light and energy appeared. It bravely
propelled at the Dark Glider. The Dark Glider …
exploded into a pear of flames.
'Leo,' Leo silently appeared.

Joshua Unsworth (10)
Killisick Junior School, Nottingham

135

Surprise, Surprise

Two girls went camping in the forest. It was creepy. They walked on leaves, twigs and stones. Sounds freaked them out, so they turned on their torches. They couldn't believe their eyes. They were so excited. They found some precious jewels and bought a beautiful mansion and they lived happily.

Tiarna Ellis (10)
Killisick Junior School, Nottingham

The Haunted House

I slowly went to the front door and knocked.
A light came on. I thought to myself, *why am I here?* I heard someone come down the creaky stairs. A man opened the door with a knife in his hand.
'Come in,' said my uncle, 'tea's on the table.'

Eden Walker (9)
Killisick Junior School, Nottingham

137

A Spooky Story

I walked up to the deserted house. Suddenly a light appeared. Then I saw the dark figure. A terrible storm began. I had to go inside. I heard a vicious laugh. I turned around but the dark figure was blocking my exit. I fainted. When I awoke I was home.

Joshua Butler (9)
Killisick Junior School, Nottingham

The Shock

I was in my house. It was raining and it was night-time. Suddenly the light turned off, I was scared. There was only me in the house. I walked upstairs and I looked in the mirror. I saw somebody. I was shivering. What a relief, it's only my reflection.

Chloe Ball (9)
Killisick Junior School, Nottingham

The Nightmare In The Rotting House

Once there was a bunch of nasty girls. I had no one.
'Go in the house,' they said.
'Well er … ' I stared at it.
The door slammed open and creaked. They pushed me in and they ran off. I looked around, I saw a girl. We became best friends.

Katy Wiltshire (9)
Killisick Junior School, Nottingham

The Haunted House

I walked up the drive then it started to rain. I went into the house, it was dusty and dark. A dog was at the top of the stairs. I saw a light, someone was in the house. I wondered who it was. I quickly ran off out the door.

Nathan Swann (8)
Killisick Junior School, Nottingham

A Day On Your Own

'Mum, Dad, where are you?'
The door blew open as I approached it, it
got louder and louder. An old pale hand
approached the door handle. *Squeak, squeak,*
what was that? I don't know. Something
grabbed my hands, pulled me in the kitchen.
'Help'
'Surprise!' It's Mum and Dad.

Adam Swann (11)
Killisick Junior School, Nottingham

142

The Figure In The House

Emma watched Luke walk in … the spooky house. She saw a figure in the window. The lights flashed on. It vanished. Emma grabbed Carly to take her to the house.
'Luke?' He was dead on the floor. There was blood everywhere. Carly went upstairs to stab the ghost. Luke awoke!

Chloe Lee (10)
Killisick Junior School, Nottingham

The Haunted School

'Help!' Creepy sounds came from the haunted school across the road. Silence came ... 'Help! The noise kept on appearing. Leanne and Franqui crept into the school ... *Bang!* Leanne died and blood squirted everywhere out of her. Suddenly Franqui woke and found herself chained to her bed.
It wasn't a dream.

Sammantha Anderson (9)
Killisick Junior School, Nottingham

Perseus And The Terrible Beast

Perseus was getting ready for the battle but a giant mythical beast stormed out of the cave! Perseus pointed the sword at the beast. The beast tried to punch Perseus but he dived away. He rolled and swiped the beast's leg off. The beast started limping. He dropped down dead.

Warren Bingley (10)
Killisick Junior School, Nottingham

The Mythical Beast!

It was a stormy night. The beast sucked all the light out of the city. People were begging the hero to kill the beast ... Perseus must kill the beast!
Zeus, God of all gods shot his lightning bolt at the horn on the beast's back.
Bang! The light was back.

Adam Harvey (10)
Killisick Junior School, Nottingham

Perseus And The Beast

There was suffering in the world. Perseus thought it was his fault, but it was the beast's fault. Perseus sprinted after the beast to kill him. Perseus found the beast, he was so mad. He stabbed him in the head, slicing it in half, but was the beast really dead?

Shaun Ball (10)
Killisick Junior School, Nottingham

147

The Gloomy Night

It was a gloomy night, everything was truly pitch-black. Suddenly a person screamed, 'Argh!'
Something happened, *bang!* Then the hand was trembling, then the person ran into the lift. It kept stopping and stopping. It was spooky. Finally the lift broke and it tumbled all the way down.

Rebecca Gee (10)
Killisick Junior School, Nottingham

The War

It was a gloomy, terrifying night. *Bang! Bang! Bang!* Red blood was everywhere, people were dead and only one person was not covered in blood. No one dared to run away. It was the biggest war in history. Something came really close …

'Derek, get off the PS2!' shouted his mum.

Jack Stott (9)
Killisick Junior School, Nottingham

149

The Monster House

There was a house! A really scary house that an evil man lived in.
One day David was bouncing his ball. It landed on his garden but he didn't dare go on it.
Suddenly … the gigantic house came alive. It ran down the road after him. Then … he was dead!

Ciara Wetton (10)
Killisick Junior School, Nottingham

Saucer Eyes

Willow had a huge pig whose eyes were as big as saucers. She named him Saucer Eyes. He met a female pig and fell in love. So whenever Willow went anywhere, Saucer Eyes wouldn't follow.
Willow got very angry with him one day and ate him for breakfast.

Olivia Choudhury (10)
Leicester High School, Leicester

It's Too Late

I run towards Ruby. She is hanging off a cliff on a piece of rock. She cries for help. I try to call the fire brigade but there is no signal. It's too late. She has gone.

Nicole Chahal (11)
Leicester High School, Leicester

The Haunted House

John entered the large, dark and gloomy house. He smiled, convinced it wasn't haunted. But not realising the door had locked behind him, a voice echoed. He wasn't so sure anymore.

Alice Butt (11)
Leicester High School, Leicester

The End

In the graveyard a twig snapped. She looked around, no one was there. She heard a strange noise. She heard moaning. The girl was scared. Something moved behind her. She felt warm breath on her neck. People in the village heard a scream and she was never ever seen again.

Rachel Bretherton (11)
Leicester High School, Leicester

The Visit

The yard was dark. There were no stars twinkling in the black sky. A small girl crept silently across the gravel path. She turned into the barn, and went into one of the stables. She lovingly stroked the palomino pony in front of her. 'Hello Gold Dust,' she said, smiling.

Laura Bateman (11)
Leicester High School, Leicester

Winston Hall

There was no turning back, I had agreed to go into the empty dilapidated Winston Hall. I crept into the lounge. A tapestry hung from the wall and behind it was a message *Beware Of The Weeping Angel And Duck!* And there in the garden was the weeping angel.

Ruby Ablett (11)
Leicester High School, Leicester

Primrose And Violet

Primrose and Violet went to see their grandma.
They bumped into loads of their friends but
never got to their grandma.
After meeting the frog, cat, mouse and wolf they
were never seen again. Where were they?

Dimple Visram (11)
Leicester High School, Leicester

The Pixie

Jasmine came home, there was an odd noise.
She went to her room.
'Hi!'
Jasmine turned. 'What are you?' She looked at
the miniature person.
'I'm a pixie!'
'What are you doing here?'
'Looking for my hat.'
'I'll help.'
Jasmine found his hat and said goodbye to her
new friend.

Avneet Mattu (11)
Leicester High School, Leicester

The Disaster

I got to my house as quickly as I could, but just found out that she had died.
The next day I went to the shop and complained about my doll, so after that I lived happily ever after, just me and my new dolly. My mum left us alone.

Nawel Hussain (11)
Leicester High School, Leicester

The Story Of Poppies And Penny

So there she was, Penny, I mean, just walking through the valley of poppies when suddenly she ducked. I saw it, it was funny, one minute she was there, then she wasn't. She had fallen down into a dip in the grass that a rabbit had started … but didn't finish.

Amelia Eatough (11)
Leicester High School, Leicester

Silly Sausage

Sausage, cold in the supermarket, must escape from nasty bacon, very nasty, mean bacon. Sausage then jumps, quick hide under this round black shield. Somebody buys the round shield.
Owner opens bag, says, 'What a lovely frying pan.'
Sausage hasn't escaped, found then fried, what a very silly sausage!

Abi Stainer (8)
Little Hill Primary School, Leicester

What An Experience!

Terrified, he slowly poured the last ingredient into the massive black cauldron. 'This will be magnificent, I shall be rich.' The mad scientist was making the most extraordinary invention - an everlasting *goldmine*. He waited nervously, suddenly it started to bubble, *whizz, bang!* Woken with a wicked, deadly, frightening idea.

Makayla Askew (9)
Loddington CE Primary School, Kettering

Chocolate Cake

When I went to sleep I heard a noise so I crept downstairs and then I heard another noise. This time it was coming from the kitchen. When I went in I saw my dad eating chocolate cake. Greedy man, it was my chocolate cake.

Shahina Ali
Medway Community Primary School, Leicester

Help!

I went to the shopping centre to buy some clothes. Then after, I went to McDonald's and all of a sudden a man dropped to the floor and had a fit. I didn't know what to do. He was vomiting blood and saying, 'Help me!' Quickly I called the ambulance.

Aleah Francis-Neale (11)
Medway Community Primary School, Leicester

The Call

Me and my friends were playing at the park when we saw two gang members kicking a man. I asked my friends, 'Get the phone quick.' They gave the phone to me and I dialled 999. When the gang members heard the police siren, the gang members ran off.

Rovena Musiqi (11)
Medway Community Primary School, Leicester

Ghost

There was a girl called Sarah. She was walking past a haunted house. Suddenly she saw a ghost, the ghost was making her get scared. She screamed and she ran. The ghost was after her. The ghost caught her. She opened her door, it was Sarah's mum. She was scared.

Shamina Choudhury (11)
Medway Community Primary School, Leicester

American Dragon Vs Kim Possible
Part 2 - The Fight

At 11.05am Jake and Kim had an argument and it ended up that Kim said we would have a fight at lunchtime. Everyone in school couldn't wait for the fight.
12 noon, they were going to have a fight but they said, 'Forget it.'

Ceanna McLarty (11)
Medway Community Primary School, Leicester

167

A Trip To The Hairdressers

'Let's go to the hairdressers,' said Rose. 'My hair needs a cut, it so long.'
'OK,' said Kate. 'I might have a haircut too.'
'I think I'll have mine feathered,' Rose said to the hairdresser.
It looked beautiful. 'I love it,' said Rose.
'It suits you,' Katie said.

Iffat Islam (11)
Medway Community Primary School, Leicester

168

Cyclops

A huge light burst through my bedroom and there right in front of me stood a huge, amazing furious Cyclops with a huge beady eye. He searched through my bedroom. The huge Cyclops grabbed my best ornament and vanished in a wisp of smoke. I stood perplexed like a statue.

Simra Ahmed (11)
Medway Community Primary School, Leicester

My Ill Teacher

Our teacher was ill and we had a supply teacher. She came to school the next day and said, 'How was your day yesterday?' We said we had fun and she was happy.

Shorifa Choudhoury (11)
Medway Community Primary School, Leicester

The Swamp Creature

'Sam! Come on,' screamed Mat.
Sam and Mat wanted to go to the swamp
because the day before, when they were
walking back from school, they went past the
swamp. Mat saw someone drowning in the dirty
swamp water. When Mat and Sam reached the
swamp, someone was there.

Hussain Bhimani (11)
Medway Community Primary School, Leicester

171

An Accident That Happened

My body shivered like I was going to die. I called out and said, 'Stop,' but it was too late. But luckily the person survived.

Zaynab Mussa (11)
Medway Community Primary School, Leicester

A Big Change

'Wow!' screamed Asher! He found himself
becoming Father Christmas. He went
downstairs and asked his parents,
'Am I dreaming?'
Dad said, 'Shall I pinch you to make sure?'
'Yes,' replied Ahser.
We went upstairs and looked in the mirror and
found out it wasn't true.

Raeesa Ahmed (11)
Medway Community Primary School, Leicester

That Party!

The house was collapsing as I ran out. Just as I got out, it fell down. I heard sirens as my friends went into the ambulance. This party ended in a disaster. Everybody's parents came to collect their children. Police came to investigate what happened, but nobody knew that day.

Ellen Zurek (11)
Medway Community Primary School, Leicester

The Alien Visit To Earth

The aliens had visited every planet in space except Earth. They are going to visit it today. The aliens have landed.

Sarfaraaz Saleh (10)
Medway Community Primary School, Leicester

Little Red Riding Hood (Retold)

Once Little Red Riding Hood thought she would take a lovely picnic for herself and her nan so she started to walk to her nan's. The wolf overheard her and sneaked to Nan's and gobbled her up. Then she walked in and screamed, picked up an axe and sliced him.

Sam Luther
North Scarle Primary School, Lincoln

World Destruction

The ground pulled me down, breathing was too
much. Death, I have never witnessed but as the
soil poured down I realised this was the end.
Years, months, days had gone but I rose again
and now the world will die, not me.
Those people will suffer, I will reign.

Kitty Waite (11)
North Scarle Primary School, Lincoln

Do You Believe In Aliens?

'You believe in aliens?'
'Yes.'
'I don't, no proof.'
'You really don't get out do you?'
'No, I have a spaceship.'
'Good joke!'
'Let's go in it then.'
'OK.'
Out of the corner of my eye, a green ray, was
he really right?

Max Chapple (10)
North Scarle Primary School, Lincoln

178

The Computer Frog

I am a magician, I am in my science lab, I cast a spell on a frog. The frog turned into a computer and said, 'Please enter your password.' I entered *abracadabra - please turn back*. The spell exploded and the frog came back alive and he was a ribbetting clown.

Jordon Mann (9)
North Scarle Primary School, Lincoln

Three Little Wolves

Once upon a time there were three little wolves. They were going to make three houses made of wood, straw and bricks. The three wolves went and got wood, straw and bricks. They built their homes. Then a big pig came and blew down their new houses.

Thomas Kinsley (10)
North Scarle Primary School, Lincoln

A Minnie Spell

I'm Minnie Witch, I made a spell. It had vinegar, toes and all sorts. I was having lunch then I heard a *bang, crash and bump*. So I rushed down, it was messy, but then I thought I could make another spell to clean it up. But … made it a lot messier.

Bryony Lawrie (9)
North Scarle Primary School, Lincoln

The Magic Potion

My village is extremely large. I'm going to have magic spells to make people thin. I'll be famous,
The ingredients are in the bowl. I drink the magic potion. I look in the cracked mirror. Nothing has happened, *bang, bang.* I look around.
Oops … my village has mysteriously disappeared.

Tamarind Russell-Webster (10)
North Scarle Primary School, Lincoln

The Journey Of A Marshmallow

I am a marshmallow from a potion. I just came down a throat. It was like I was in the ocean but I didn't have a boat. I live in Haribo, wrapped with Olympic-sized mallows but now I'm in someone's stomach and have to paddle in the shallows.

Grace Gourley (10)
North Scarle Primary School, Lincoln

Little Miss Muffet

I was walking on the pavement, I saw a little girl.
I stopped and asked, 'What's your name?'
She replied, 'Miss Muffet.'
Then I said, 'My name is Courtney.'
She was eating porridge when all of a sudden
a spider came down beside her and scared her
away.
Argh!

Courtney Danby (10)
St Edward's CE Primary School, Derby

Three Blind Mice

I was walking down the road and I saw three blind mice and they ran into a woman's house. She chased them away with a big meat axe to try and cut off their tails but they got away and I said, 'Ha, ha.'

Alex Corson (9)
St Edward's CE Primary School, Derby

Football Day

I went to the park to play football and I was in goal. I was with my mates. We were winning 4-0.
The players were Sophie, Sam and Jake.
It was 7 o'clock, we had to go home so we all rushed the game and went back home quickly!

Kristian Garner (10)
St Edward's CE Primary School, Derby

Untitled

I was walking through the forest and smelt some porridge. I followed it and it led me to a house, a great big house. So anyway, I went in and there was three bowls of porridge. I ate it and it was yummy. The bears came home, I ran.

Lydia Baxter (10)
St Edward's CE Primary School, Derby

The Painful Dog

I went to call for my friend. I went up a hill and about halfway up a dog came charging at me and bit me.
In thirty minutes I was at the hospital and had a tetanus jab and it hurt really badly.

Kyle Dabell (10)
St Edward's CE Primary School, Derby

The Zoo

I went to the zoo one day and saw an elephant.
It trumped and gassed everyone out so we
went to see the monkey but it was picking his
nose. So we went to see giraffes but they had
very long tongues which licked me. Horrid zoo.

Sophie Wiggins (10)
St Edward's CE Primary School, Derby

189

Tokyo Drift

One night there was a racing car driver. He was racing in a building site. There was a short cut, he went down it and almost got in front of his opponent but he lost control. They both crashed badly into the bollard and stopped. After, they were in hospital.

Joshua Finney (10)
St Edward's CE Primary School, Derby

My Cat

My cat Angel was walking down the road when
he spotted some mice. He ran as fast as he
could and pounced on them. They ran into a
fence and made him get stuck.
He finally got free. He climbed up a tree and
saw the mice and made friends.

Rebekah Atkinson (9)
St Edward's CE Primary School, Derby

Doctor Who?

The alien had landed on Earth.
'Quick, quick, run! It's catching us up,' said
Scott in a frightened voice. He tried to hide.
Suddenly he saw something moving in the
shadows. 'Who's that?' said Scott.
'I'm the Doctor, Doctor Who.'
'Wake up Scott, it's the Doctor,' said Mum.
'Doctor Who?'

Scott Comery
St Edward's CE Primary School, Derby

My Leg

I was in the playground. I slipped and hurt my leg. I went to have a look at it and I had a big cut. I showed the teacher and she gave me an ice pack. When I got home, I showed my mum and dad and my brother Stuart.

Jessica Reddish (10)
St Edward's CE Primary School, Derby

The BMW M3 GTR

One night a BMW was speeding down the motorway at 100 miles an hour making a roaring noise. He was in the fast lane, racing his rival. The rival was a Dodge Viper GTS R, swerving around traffic, making cars slow down.
Eventually the Dodge crashed and the BMW won.

Nathan Moffatt (10)
St Edward's CE Primary School, Derby

194

Annoying Talking Animal

Hi my name is Donkey and this morning in the forest I saw a big, fat, ugly ogre. And guess what? He saved my life. You know that is pretty amazing for an ogre. We ended up being mates but then I met a fire-breathing dragon.

Megan Archer (10)
St Edward's CE Primary School, Derby

String Ball

Waking up from a long winter's catnap, I started
to approach my vicious prey.
After a while the prey starts to make a sudden
move. The fight starts with a *ding-dong*. I
pounce on the other opponent, it's on the floor.
The referee shouts, 'The cat is the winner!'

Laura Powell (10)
St John Fisher RC Primary School, Wigston

The Curse Of The Vase

Bang! A figure came down the chimney. He touched a vase my mum bought and shot up the chimney.

The next day I looked at the vase. It belonged to a man in 1803 called Gary Arkson, he'd been murdered.

I looked up and saw blood dripping from the vase!

Harry Naylor
St John Fisher RC Primary School, Wigston

The Dagger

'Stick the dagger in his neck!' he screeched!
Yuck, blood gushing everywhere.
'Miss I feel sick, I didn't feel that well anyway,'
she stuttered.
'Look Mr Gallagher is that gory or what?'
(Boys typical).
'Yeah great!' he said sickly.
'Turn the TV off now.'
'Sorry for any disturbance caused.'

Atlanta Hackshaw
St John Fisher RC Primary School, Wigston

Scary Story

'Mum, Mum, the monsters are attacking.'
'What! Get out of the house now.'
'But Mum, the monsters are coming up the stairs.'
'Climb out the window.'
'Mum, we're surrounded.'
'Run, don't look back son, just keep running.'
The monsters were coming even closer.
'Can you read me that story tomorrow?'

Joseph Tomlin (10)
St John Fisher RC Primary School, Wigston

Whizz, Pop, Bang!

I'm standing here watching the most important science experiment of the century. What will happen? I pour the final ingredient into the jug. Will it work? The atmosphere in the room is tense!

Suddenly, *bang,* black clouds of smoke start puffing out of the container. It had gone terribly wrong.

Christopher Donaghey (10)
St John Fisher RC Primary School, Wigston

My First Time On MSN!

Turning on the computer to start MSN I was thinking who I should add. MSN came up on the computer screen and I clicked on the sign at the bottom. It signed me in - yeh! So I started to add my friends' email addresses like Kalen, Eilidh, Emma and Annabelle.

Sophie Angrave
St John Fisher RC Primary School, Wigston

201

Born

When the spring smell was in the air and I was
tight inside a squirmy case, inside an animal
with black stripes and orange fur and then my
mother stopped and out I came like something
falling out of a bag that was unzipped.

David Astill (10)
St John Fisher RC Primary School, Wigston

It Never Rains, It Pours

Water in your wellies and everywhere in your house, it never rains, it pours. Floating cars and sinking boats, rain is crashing on the windows. Water is flooding through the doors and I can feel my toes go numb. We can only wait and keep hoping that someone will come.

Eilidh Squire (10)
St John Fisher RC Primary School, Wigston

A Boy's First Food Fight

Our normal lunchtime everybody's happy eating their lunch then suddenly a Pukka pie placed its face on my poor innocent head. Then I stood up straight and picked up a burger with extra ketchup, I lobbed it. *Wheeee,* then *splash!* As it landed on the head teacher's head. *Busted!*

Derry Foran
St John Fisher RC Primary School, Wigston

George Vs Tony Blair

We're in the last minute of time and it is still George 0, Tony Blair 0! George is in possession, he charges up the pitch, he flicks it up and volleys it into the top corner. The final whistle goes! George has won the FA Cup, An amazing victory.

George Zubryckyj
St John Fisher RC Primary School, Wigston

205

Famous Eyes

I didn't think I'd ever be famous but one day I read a mysterious book like no other. I thought I had no talent whatsoever. Then I read the book I'd found.
A week later, I was famous …

Giulia Gilmore
St John Fisher RC Primary School, Wigston

Crash Down!

Looking out the window over the sea is a flying thing! Suddenly a light came on. I put my seatbelt on.
'We're going down,' someone said.
I got my parachute and jumped. I gently hit the ground. 'Help!'
I was in a sharp mouth. Now I'm in a T-rex.

Alex Hunt (10)
St John Fisher RC Primary School, Wigston

207

Orchestra

Scared, but excitedly, I began to play some terrible notes. *Squeak, toot, squeak!* The teacher screamed at me because I played the notes horrendously but I think I did well as it is my first day. Oh well, maybe I'll do better next time. Until then, I should keep practising.

Daniel Richmond
St John Fisher RC Primary School, Wigston

My First Flight

I'm only small, only a chick, 3 and a half months old and I'm going to fly! Slowly I stumbled to the edge of the cliff and opened my fluffy wings out wide, dangling my wing. I finally took off waving my wings, I climbed.
Eventually I found a lovely place to land.

James Harnedy (9)
St John Fisher RC Primary School, Wigston

The Labyrinth Horn

I am in the labyrinth, the Minotaur is in here somewhere, but where … wait! I hear footsteps! Hey … the footsteps are getting louder and louder, *rrrooooaaarrrr! Argh!*
My brother wakes me with a football horn. I am so mad, nevertheless, he did wake me up from the nightmare,
Wow!

Stephen Cattermole (10)
St John Fisher RC Primary School, Wigston

The Cave Nobody Comes Out Of!

Teeth as big as icebergs, claws as sharp as knives. Slowly I crawled away, banging into the door of the cave, there's no escape! Where do I run? Where do I hide? More to the point, what is that pongy smell? And oh no, no it's about to *ahhh!*

Chloe Shelton (10)
St John Fisher RC Primary School, Wigston

Jamie's Desire

Soaring through the blistering winds and trudging through scalding deserts was a young boy named Jamie.

Jamie's desire was to climb to the top of Mount Everest with his dad Bernie.

'Hey Jamie wake up, you're going to miss the bus!'

It was only a dream, or was it?

Emma Carpenter (10)
St John Fisher RC Primary School, Wigston

Overactive Imagination

I felt my neck prickle but I daren't look. My hairs on my arms stood up. I felt a gust of wind on my neck but I daren't look. I wish I didn't have an overactive imagination when I watch a horror movie. I absolutely and completely hate it.

Joe Donoghue (9)
St John's CE Primary School, Belper

Up, Up And Down!

Tom was incredibly nervous. He was just about
to travel high in the sky. He strapped himself in.
He waited. Tom was going up and up.
He was scared,
'Ten, nine, eight,' he counted.
He plunged down and was upside down.
It was the best roller coaster ever.

Josh Weston (10)
St John's CE Primary School, Belper

214

Timmy And His Dog

'I want a dog,' yelled Timmy.
'No!' Mum shouted.
'Yes!' Timmy yelled.
'Bed!' yelled Mum.
In the night Timmy dreamt he had a dog.
The next morning Timmy went to breakfast.
'I've a surprise!' said Mum.
Timmy followed her and there was a tiny puppy.
'Wow, thanks,' said Timmy speechlessly.

Amy Robinson (10)
St John's CE Primary School, Belper

Some Science Is Boring ... But Not All

This was it, sweat was running down my face, my arms were shaking. The first attempt to make time travel possible was now. It must work but the evil science teacher had come. He was smashing the controls.
'Wake up Ben! This is a science lesson, not your bedroom!'

Ben Hext (10)
St John's CE Primary School, Belper

216

Oblivion

I was strapped in, exactly 50 foot above ground level. My heart was pumping at astonishing speed. I suddenly tipped and was going down to the ground at what felt like 300mph. I thought that was it, gone forever.
Suddenly I heard a *shh* and I was standing on ground.

Brad Reed (10)
St John's CE Primary School, Belper

It's Coming Closer

I'm swimming really happily but then a shark
comes from behind.
A ship, it's coming closer, so close, then snap!
'Emily stop daydreaming, we're getting this
pool.'

Emily Stephenson (10)
St John's CE Primary School, Belper

Explosion

In school we had a science day. I wanted to do lots of things like make a light switch so I did. But all of a sudden something dreadful happened. I had accidentally spilt my drink all over my light switch. It started bubbling, then *bang!* Explosion!
Oops, ha, ha!

Ellis Wakelin (10)
St John's CE Primary School, Belper

Untitled

One dark stormy night a boy arrived home for his tea. Then suddenly there was not time for tea. It was time to go on holiday.
When he and his family got on the plane it started to move 20, 40, 60, 80, 100mph, I was terrified, then take-off!

Josh Chrich (10)
St John's CE Primary School, Belper

The Dragon Nightmare

A bright golden dragon was sleeping. Tim went into the cavern. There were lots of sparkling jewels and gold. Tim nicked an emerald as green as grass. The dragon awoke. Tim ran for it. The dragon was soaring above, faster than the speed of sound. Then Tim awoke, frightened!

Matthew Pike (10)
St John's CE Primary School, Belper

Why Do We Have To Go To School?

Abbie and James walked down the path. Across the road there was a great looming building. As they crossed the road a shrill bell began to ring. Abbie and James ran to the building. When they got there Abbie sighed and said, 'Why do we have to go to school?'

Frances Devine (10)
St Mary's Catholic Primary School, Loughborough

Horror In The Doorway

Ollie stared at the door. Soon he would be able to have his heart's desire. He crept through the squeaky door. There it was, bulging with lovely cash.

Then it happened, in the doorway stood a horrid, ugly figure, so awful, Ollie screamed in fright,

'Oliver,' shouted his fuming dad.

Ben Godber (10)
St Mary's Catholic Primary School, Loughborough

223

Strange

The house was silent, no lights on or anything, pitch-black all around then a door creaked! I could hear footsteps getting louder, coming closer. A hand touched my shoulder. I opened my mouth to scream but I was too late, the thing had already caught me - *argh*!

Beckie Leigh Booth (11)
St Mary's CE Primary School, Melton Mowbray

Mum And Dad's Party!

It was late! The telly was on. It was on full blast but I could still hear the party below. Suddenly the telly went off. There was a scream in the lounge. Everyone stood amazed. There had been a murder! Nobody told me that it was a murder mystery party!

Evangeline Wood (11)
St Mary's RC Primary School, High Peak

Prince Not- So- Charming Spoils The Day

Along Prince Charming rode, his hair blowing in the wind.
'My darling!' Rapunzel called from the tower, arms outstretched. 'You've come to save me!'
He paused. 'Sorry babe, just got a call from Sleeping Beauty, she's in a jam on the A6, got to be all heroic and that … cheerio!'

Kathrine Payne (11)
St Mary's RC Primary School, High Peak

The Aliens

My house is over a graveyard, it's so creepy. I fell asleep one night just for about an hour, then *kaboom!* It woke me up … so … confusing. I didn't know what it was so I walked to my window.

'Aliens,' I closed my eyes, opened them, the aliens had gone.

Rhiannan Frost (9)
St Mary's RC Primary School, High Peak

The Strange Mixture

The professor was sat in his lab, mixing strange looking chemicals. *I've almost got it,* he thought. 'Now,' he said, looking around. He stood up and started shuffling through shelves of glass bottles. 'Aha!' He grabbed a purple bottle and added it to the mixture. *Bang!* The professor disappeared.

Emily Brown (10)
St Mary's RC Primary School, High Peak

What Is Home?

I have never had a home, I am an orphan and I live in an orphanage, drowned in self pity. The door creaks open. It's the woman who looks after me.

'Molly, you're being adopted!'

I say a silent prayer of thanks to God and walk into my new life.

Isabelle Kenyon (11)
St Mary's RC Primary School, High Peak

Falling Down

I'm now on my broom flying, when suddenly I crash into a rock-hard wall. I gradually fall and hit the surface. I have bruises and dripping blood everywhere. Everyone rushes towards me and the ambulance speeds me to the hospital. I awake after five hours and can't remember anything.

Chloe Pearce (10)
St Thomas' Primary School, Boston

Spooky Skeletons

I walked down into the deep darkness of the cellar, when suddenly I spotted two things that were rather strange. They looked white and big. They were skeletons. 'Quick run!' I shouted. The sun shone and the skeletons vanished into thin air.

Harry Bunce (10)
St Thomas' Primary School, Boston

Bonfire Night

One night, Bonfire Night, you could see the bonfire from miles off. The bonfire crackled in the gusty wind. All the people watched in amazement as the fireworks shot up like bombs. They screamed up, *bang!* they exploded in the air in a multitude of colours. Pure magic!

Ryan Lawson (10)
St Thomas' Primary School, Boston

Winnie The Witch

I popped over to Winnie's house, until rumour
had it she was a witch.
I'd never seemed to notice her pointed hat and
broomstick and strange growing flower in the
garden. A black pot sat in the middle of her
room.
I think the rumour's right. Winnie's a *witch!*

Jessica Lucas (10)
St Thomas' Primary School, Boston

The Big Bang!

Bang! It had all disappeared. Where?
'Mum it's going to blow up, it's boiling in here.
Quick!' screamed Ivy violently at her mother.
Suddenly a bang was heard all over the
gigantic new city. Then people rushed quietly
at the exploded house. *Bang! Bang! Bang!* into
the eternal mist!

Lewis Smith (10)
St Thomas' Primary School, Boston

234

Arctic Weather

I was shivering to death. The snow drifted to the ground silently. As it got thicker, I wished that I'd never journeyed to the Arctic. A polar bear walked towards me, and it seemed to say follow me. I did, and the next thing I knew, I was back home.

Katie Gray (10)
St Thomas' Primary School, Boston

The Failed Quest

Candles flickered, making shadows crawl and slither. A titter vibrated through the somewhat sickly atmosphere. Scampering, panting. The immaculate floor shook as they ran. A hovering piece of wood appeared that contained a riddle. Patience was dwindling, still paying attention to the riddle.

But then … footprints. Grabbed. Gone. Silence!

Jennifer Brown (9)
St Thomas' Primary School, Boston

Ghost Train

Dusty cobwebs brushed my hair as I entered the horrible place. Spooky sounds came closer. Lightning struck, making me jump. Skeletons flew out of the walls into my face, red lights all around. Then, a ticking noise started, *tick, tick, tick. Bang!* The doors burst open. The nightmare was over.

Thomas Crook (10)
St Thomas' Primary School, Boston

Sniffing Flowers

The shimmering sun sparkled splendidly.
The thousand flowers smelling marvellous.
I sniffed the first gold-coloured flower then
zap! I couldn't smell anymore. I couldn't smell
another splendid flower ever, ever again.
The soft touch of my fingertips was all I had left.

Alice Sands (10)
St Thomas' Primary School, Boston

Spirits In The Church

It was mid-summer and there was a wedding on in the village church. I listened to the voice of the vicar. Suddenly the voice had disappeared. I opened the creaky wooden door and entered the mysterious church. *Bang!* The door was taken out of my hand and shut. *Dead!*

Laura Kirk (10)
St Thomas' Primary School, Boston

New Life

Still golden, it was wedged in the damp grass.
A perfectly formed egg. Suddenly a miniature
crack travelled down it. A tiny beak pointed out
and weakly cheeped. Its exhausted body lay
quietly in the broken shell. A miraculous baby
chick, searching for a caring mother.

Sarah Rudge (10)
St Thomas' Primary School, Boston

Countdown From Sixty

'Kate, could you come in for a minute?' Sophie
shouted from her office.
I retraced my steps backwards and walked
through the bright blue door. In front of me
stood a tall woman dressed in green.
'Kate, this could be your future foster parent,'
Sophie grinned.
Fifty-two, fifty-one, I thought.

Sarah Woodcock (10)
St Thomas' Primary School, Boston

The Dreaded Hairdresser

I stumbled into the shop and the scent of dead rats drifted my way. The horrid Marane sat me down upon a chair. I waited for the pain to start … *Arrgghh!* I felt the scissors upon my head attacking everything.

Then Marane kicked me out, with hair like a poodle.

Kirstie Herd (10)
St Thomas' Primary School, Boston

242

The Day It Happened

Lola was near school. She was getting annoyed with the weather and her sister. She went into school and on the marked floor she found a blue pencil. She picked it up and it suddenly stopped raining, she looked around for her sister but she wasn't there. It was quiet.

Claire Broad (11)
Shelthorpe Community School, Loughborough

Past Life

Merissa's day was about to change when she embarked on a dangerous journey into the past. She found out who she was in her past life. She was a wanted criminal, but she stole for good. Merissa had to find a way to her own time in the present.

Jessica Frew (11)
Shelthorpe Community School, Loughborough

Where Is Everybody?

Josh went out for a walk as he was very bored inside. He went to call for his best friend Shayne; but when he got there, Shayne's house was empty. In fact everywhere Josh went, no one was there. Josh ran home more frightened than ever. But …

Nicole-Jade Driver (11)
Shelthorpe Community School, Loughborough

Duskpull And His Friend Uchip

Duskpull and Uchip were both good guys and Tyrain was their arch enemy.
One day Duskpull and Uchip faced the bad guy Tyrain, who was a dragon as well as a lizard. Duskpull attacked first. He hit Tyrain in the head and then Uchip attacked and they both killed him together.

James Suffolk (11)
Shelthorpe Community School, Loughborough

246

Silly Me

I was alone while swimming in the cool blue sea, with the waves crashing against the rocks. Suddenly, the water was swirling and noises started happening … Of course, I fell asleep in the bath and my mum pulled the plug out and my brother pulled the toilet chain – silly me!

Ella Lucas (9)
Tansley Primary School, Matlock

The Dream

I went to the beach. I went into the sea and I saw the Loch Ness monster. It tried to get me. I was very scared, but it was just a dream. I kept dreaming about it every night, but one night I did not have that dream.

Ruby Stones (6)
Theddlethorpe Primary School, Mablethorpe

248

The Spooky Castle

It was a rainy night and me, Katie and Frances wanted to go into the spooky castle.
We went in the castle and saw Jazmine and Faye. Suddenly we saw a ghost. It jumped up, and the sheet fell off, it was Mollie.

Ayisha Bassham (6)
Theddlethorpe Primary School, Mablethorpe

A Calm Blue Sea?

One day I went diving in a calm blue sea. When suddenly I saw a shark coming towards me. I swam away as quickly as I could. My heart was beating faster and faster. Would I be tea for this shark? No, it was only a cardboard box.

Elliot Peers (7)
Theddlethorpe Primary School, Mablethorpe

A Very Wet Day

I was at school with my friends. It started to rain. It rained and rained. It flooded. It was a good job I had brought some goggles. We all swam home. I said, 'Yes, no more school today!'

Katherine Wood (7)
Theddlethorpe Primary School, Mablethorpe

Shark Attack

The waves were calm. Out of the water, a great white shark rocked the boat. The shark jumped out of the water. A mighty splash covered the boat. The shark lifted its head onto the boat. A minute later, its head was under the water again. But had it gone?

Jess Matthews (7)
Theddlethorpe Primary School, Mablethorpe

Teddy's Adventures

I took my teddy to the seaside. I dropped my teddy in the sea. A shark escaped from the zoo and came to rip my teddy in half. I was sad. My gran and my mum bought me a new teddy.

Tristan Prince (6)
Theddlethorpe Primary School, Mablethorpe

The Slam

My brother came home from kick boxing and the door slammed. He thought that there was a monster. He was ready to kick box. His hands were shaking and he was scared. His arms were shaking and his legs were shaking. It was just the wind.

Cullum Perry (7)
Theddlethorpe Primary School, Mablethorpe

254

My Worst Nightmare

'Help! Help!' I ran as fast as I could. It was following me. 'Mum, Mum!' I shouted as I jumped on my bed. It came into the room. I grabbed a cover. Mum ran into the room. 'Be nice to your baby cousin Nathan.'
'OK Mum. I will,' I sighed.

Mollie Wyllie (8)
Theddlethorpe Primary School, Mablethorpe

255

In The Dark Park

Alex was walking through the park. It started to get darker. The trees started to bend their branches down to touch the floor. Alex was lost. He clawed his way through the dense jungle. He was lost, scratched to bits and started crying.

'It's just a video Sam,' laughed Mum.

Alex Orthodoxou (8)
Theddlethorpe Primary School, Mablethorpe

The Escaped Elephant

Once I was walking in a jungle when I heard
a strange noise. It sounded like something
was following me. Something grabbed me in
the trees. Water was dripping down my back.
Heavy stamping feet behind me.
It's that elephant again – he's escaped from the
zoo!
'Get back!' I shouted.

Harvey Faulkner (8)
Theddlethorpe Primary School, Mablethorpe

The New Mirror

Who was this staring at me? They had a pale
face covered in spots. Their hair was sticking
up. They were fat, with bloodshot eyes. It
looked like an alien or ghost. I thought it was
my dad, but oh no, it's just the new mirror Mum
put up.

Daniel Ramsden (9)
Theddlethorpe Primary School, Mablethorpe

The Bogeyman

Once I sneezed and a green wobbling
bogeyman appeared. I said, 'Who are you?'
'I'm the bogeyman.' He started to shake me
and pushed me around my bedroom.
I had had enough. I grabbed him in a tissue
and flushed him down the toilet.

Shaun Henderson (8)
Theddlethorpe Primary School, Mablethorpe

Aliens!

'Help, help! It's going to get me,' I cried.
A giant green and red hand came down from
the sky. It got lower and lower every time I
moved. I was sucked into a spaceship, where
everyone looked the same. What was going to
happen to me? Oh no!

Nathan Smith (8)
Theddlethorpe Primary School, Mablethorpe

The Monster

The monster is coming. I had been warned all about it. But still I was afraid. Would it destroy my room? Break all my toys? Bite me and hit me? Yell and hiss in my face? Yes, it would. I absolutely hate it when my cousin Georgina comes to stay.

Abigail Gill (9)
Theddlethorpe Primary School, Mablethorpe

The Monster Sock

I plunged my hand deep into the damp hole.
I could feel soft warm things and wet slimy
things. Then I touched something. It was all
fluffy like a monster. It was dark with spots on
it. I screamed. Carefully I pulled it out – my
mouldy football sock!

Chloe Ward (8)
Theddlethorpe Primary School, Mablethorpe

Breakfast Time

I was fast asleep dreaming about the summer holidays. Suddenly there was a huge thud and my face was covered by a furry wriggling beast. It clawed at my quilt and pushed a wet nose in my ear. Hot fishy breath blew across my face. The cat wanted his breakfast.

Tayla Anderson (8)
Theddlethorpe Primary School, Mablethorpe

The Martians Who Ate Our School

I walked down the street one morning to find the school in ruins. Then I saw some Martians eating everything. They ate the tables, they ate the chairs, they ate the teachers and spat out the hairs. They ate the cats, then went back home to Mars. Bye, bye aliens!

Liam Bradley (8)
Theddlethorpe Primary School, Mablethorpe

264

My Teacher's Torture

I trembled and shook while I got in the car.
'Why do I have to go to school?' I asked.
'Because,' said Mum. 'Right kits on!'
So I did, oh no the T-shirt and shorts were
killing me. We went on to the field. 'I'm dying!'
'It's only PE!'

Abi Wood (8)
Theddlethorpe Primary School, Mablethorpe

Untitled

The boy and girl ran up the stairs. Mum went to check, but they were gone! She told the older sister. She went to look. At last she found them behind the waterfall.

A woman came out and said, 'Leave the children!'

'No.'

So they all ran away home. *Yeaah!*

Ellie Fox (10)
Walton Holymoorside Primary School, Chesterfield

266

Untitled

One snowy, summer morning when some guy was adorning a wall. A tiny, tweeting bird perched upon my window sill and its soft sweet tune opened my heart. The bird was fragile, young and gay. It paused rapidly.
I gently pulled the window down and crushed its miniscule skull!

Jake Grisdale (10)
Walton Holymoorside Primary School, Chesterfield

The Mission

There were two creatures called Purple and Brown. Their mission was to destroy Doctor Black's generator. Doctor Black's generator terminates people into robots. So Purple and Brown surprisingly reached Doctor Black's lair and saw the distinctive generator, ran near and destroyed it. *Bam!* Purple and Brown won. They both smiled.

Alexander Hall (9)
Walton Holymoorside Primary School, Chesterfield

268

Jess And The Mission

'Maisy's gone!' screamed Jess, as she walked out the front door. Her mum gave her a magic bone which transports you to places.

Crash! 'I'm here,' yelled Jess, as she got out of the bone. Jess ran to find Maisy. 'Maisy, you're safe!' she screamed.

Bang! We're back home *Yey!*

Lauren Hamshaw (9)
Walton Holymoorside Primary School, Chesterfield

The Mission

Scuba diving down, I saw the sunken ship. I found the treasure chest and pulled with all of my might. The treasure chest became free and I swam (with a struggle) to the surface.
'Well done!' said my boss. 'You retrieved the treasure. Mission complete!' he added with a smile.

Emma Brown (11)
Walton Holymoorside Primary School, Chesterfield

270

The Attack

Two children, Alex and Matt go on a walk to the park at 7.30pm and there is a burglary happening. Alex confidently ran in with a stick to hit them, but outside Matt ran away and never came back. Alex hit them and the police took them away.

Curtis-James Marriott (10)
Walton Holymoorside Primary School, Chesterfield

The Monster

'Eric! Can I borrow your Game Boy?'
'No!'
'Fine, I'll smack you,' I cried.
'You can only play with it for ten minutes while I
go and talk to my mates,' moaned Eric.
Suddenly, while playing, the monster from the
game popped out. I got a boot and smacked it.

Wesal Mazen (10)
Walton Holymoorside Primary School, Chesterfield

272

The Mission

I'm on the beach in Italy, when suddenly someone steals my plan to take over the world. Running to my lair, I find an exterminator gun to destroy the whole world. I shoot the gun, I get shot back, but I win.
Afterwards I have a massive party. Yeah! Yeah!

Tom Hall (10)
Walton Holymoorside Primary School, Chesterfield

The Mystery

Three children. The eldest children watch TV, the youngest in bed. One child goes outside the room, other one falls asleep.
He wakes up and goes to the bathroom upstairs. Sees thing in the bath – sister jumps on him. He goes crazy. He dies.
Investigations carried out, they find nothing.

Minnie Greatorex (11)
Walton Holymoorside Primary School, Chesterfield

The Mission

Malton is down the road from a haunted castle.
Malton was planning a six day trip to the castle.
They were going to defeat ghosts.
The first night they were there, they started to
get lots of pepper to sprinkle on them.
It took five days, eventually they did it.

Chloe Stone (10)
Walton Holymoorside Primary School, Chesterfield

275

The Mission

Walking through the grassy field to Grampa's, he asked for a glowing ruby. Searching, we headed off. All day we searched.
Finally we had to rest in a stony building (a cave).
Suddenly my sister came running with a red object (the glowing ruby). We had now found it!

Laura Turner (9)
Walton Holymoorside Primary School, Chesterfield

The Diamond

Planning to steal a glistening diamond,
was Climch (he was a crook). Trying not
to be found, he stole the diamond. Luckily
Policewoman Madden cornered him, as soon
as she found out. Escaping to the sewers he
was outrun.
However the diamond was safe! Was that the
end of it?

Helen Humphries (10)
Walton Holymoorside Primary School, Chesterfield

Grizzly Situation

Ominously the letterbox creaked. Simon sprung downstairs to find out what the reason for the strange unpleasing action of the letterbox was. He couldn't make it out.
Nick peered out of the window beside the door. It was a creature by the looks of it – a bad one too!

Samuel Shaw (10)
Walton Holymoorside Primary School, Chesterfield

278

The Mission

I arrived on the shining shore of Panini Island,
fighting in World War II. The commander cruelly
announced that I would be completing a
mission by myself.
Nervously climbing up a dangerous mountain,
I eventually arrived at the German base.
Annihilating them, I soon took over. Victory's in
sight. *Yes!*

Matthew Kellett (10)
Walton Holymoorside Primary School, Chesterfield

The Day The Snake Escaped

Oh no, my bag is missing! I must get it back. It has something in it that no one else must see. Luckily the school was still open and I could get it, but it was too late, the snake had gone. It could be anywhere in this big school.

Meghan Hardy (11)
Walton Holymoorside Primary School, Chesterfield

The Mission

Alex is sixteen years old, and he is chased by a tornado that is destroying the world. He's got to find three gems in the ruins of Atlantis, to stop the tornado and save the world. He touches three objects and then … Does he save the world? Will he survive?

Luke Lipscombe (10)
Walton Holymoorside Primary School, Chesterfield

Mission Rabbits

Crash! The rabbits fell into a glade, and noticed they were surrounded by masked creatures, which burnt up in the sunlight – although they didn't know this yet.

The rabbits started on their plan. They would tackle one creature by one. They were victorious and got to the burrow safely. Yey!

Eleanor Squires (10)
Walton Holymoorside Primary School, Chesterfield

282

Gift Box

She made for the door and jumped out into the
park. Tracy wasn't far behind. 'Give me back
my bracelet!' she screamed.
Julie looked behind before vanishing into the
wall. 'Help!' screamed Julie.
'Place your gift in the box!' said a voice.
Julie put in the bracelet.
She was back!

Sam Brown (10)
Walton Holymoorside Primary School, Chesterfield

283

Lost

In an ocean, a shark called Gumi, lost his parents in a passing ship called the Titanic. He cautiously followed it.
Afterwards he met a jellyfish called Jim. The ship eventually crashed into a big iceberg and Gumi found his parents and was best friends with Jim the jellyfish.

Ross Cave (10)
Walton Holymoorside Primary School, Chesterfield

The Mystery Of The Car That Wouldn't Work

Tom got in his car. 'Oh no!' he said. 'It isn't working. It's got petrol.' He got out and walked. 'Do you know why my car isn't working?'
'No.'
He asked somebody in a car. 'Mine has got petrol and it's working.'
He went back and discovered it needed petrol.

Jacob Benson (8)
Walton Holymoorside Primary School, Chesterfield

285

Gods And Goddesses

I heard a rustle, then a growl. I saw it, a great
big Hellhound. I fell back into the river, but I
could breathe. I rose out of the water. I flew, I
became a glowing goddess. Goddess of all
good things. My parents were Zeus, Poseidon,
Aphrodite and Athena.

Kira Botham (7)
Walton Holymoorside Primary School, Chesterfield

The Square Football

Every day I go to school and play football. But today it was a square football. So I asked the teacher.
She said, 'I don't know.'
When I got the newspaper I saw the contest to see how long you can last with a square football.

Anna Stevenson (8)
Walton Holymoorside Primary School, Chesterfield

The Mystery Of The Flat Football

One lovely day I went outside to play football with William, Daniel and Charlie. We played on the field. Me and William stick Daniel and Charlie. Charlie came down the pitch, he kicked it into a bush. The ball popped. That dog popped it.
That explains the flat football.

Alex Swinden (8)
Walton Holymoorside Primary School, Chesterfield

288

The Mystery Of The Missing Pencil

The missing pencil wasn't on my desk. I looked upstairs and downstairs for my pencil and I couldn't find it anywhere.
I told Chloe to go and she said, 'Why?'
So I said, 'I want to find it.' So I found it with my dog. Yes, so yes!

Ellouise Corbridge (8)
Walton Holymoorside Primary School, Chesterfield

My Surprise Birthday

I stepped into my house. It was dark. My mum
and dad said they would be home by now.
Even the slightest creak would make me jump. I
heard something coming from the lounge.
The door burst open … 'Surprise!'
Wow what a great day!

Danielle Gatti (8)
Walton Holymoorside Primary School, Chesterfield

290

The Breeze To Nowhere

Abbey opened the window, in popped a breeze. It swept Abbey off her feet and she flew past an exotic land. She shouted the breeze to stop, but what could she do? Her mama bellowed. She heard her mama.

Suddenly the tornado stopped. Abbey fell through the chimney.

Go Abbey!

Emily Dods (9)
Walton Holymoorside Primary School, Chesterfield

The Mystery Of The Science Lab

One day there was a professor called Marvin. Marvin, had worked all of his life on one experiment. Today, at 2.00pm his computer told him to go to the lab, but when he got there, the whole thing had been destroyed.

Salvador Jimenez-Sanchez (8)
Walton Holymoorside Primary School, Chesterfield

Untitled

One day there was a pencil that never sharpened and never got blunt. One day a boy called Fred picked up the old pencil and put it in his pocket.
At lunch he felt a hot thing in his pocket. He pulled the pencil out and dropped it!

Alexander Stockton (9)
Walton Holymoorside Primary School, Chesterfield

The Monster

I entered my house. I saw something. It was
ugly, atrocious, appalling, bulgy, gobstopping.
In fact, they had to invent a whole new world for
how ugly it was.
But I will tell you what it was, my brother Finbar.

Jake Irani (9)
Walton Holymoorside Primary School, Chesterfield

294

The Mystery Of The Burnt Car

I was coming out with my friends Dan, Sam and Alex. Then we saw a burnt car. We told the police, but they died. We told our parents, they didn't believe us. But we fought. We killed them and the police came to put them in jail.

William Ball (8)
Walton Holymoorside Primary School, Chesterfield

The Haircut

Me, Katie and Anna went for a haircut. A lady
sat down. The new hair cutter cut off all her hair.
She screamed, *'Argh!'*
We quickly ran away.
'I'm not having my hair cut,' I exclaimed.
We've got to tell the old hair cutters, this is a
mystery.

Sophie Shaw (8)
Walton Holymoorside Primary School, Chesterfield

296

Warm Weather

The magic swept through the rainbow, warm
breeze tinkled the air …
The scary thunder thumped under the breeze
terrifying the bright colours. Sparkling sun
makes thunder boiling hot … it *burns!* Rainbow
freshness glows in the sky again. Lovely
laughter returns. Rainbow magic occurs to
make warm weather.

Natalie Sharratt (9)
Walton Holymoorside Primary School, Chesterfield

Zombie Surprise

In a dark house there was a dark door. There
were five scary zombies.
'Surprise! It's your surprise birthday party!'

Slater Smith (9)
Walton Holymoorside Primary School, Chesterfield

Untitled

Once I was on a journey to King Kong World but when I got there I heard a sudden sound – *roaaa!* I leaped onto a rock and got in the plane so no people would ever see King Kong again.

James Sharp (8)
Walton Holymoorside Primary School, Chesterfield

In The Middle Of The Night

It was the middle of the night. I went outside, I tripped speedily into a container. It smelt and then a rotten banana skin fell on me. The floors were very damp. I eventually got out. I never knew a bin was so horrid!

James Umney (9)
Walton Holymoorside Primary School, Chesterfield

300

Snowy Days

One day it snowed. My heart fell into my lungs, from all the fear. My earrings squeezed my ears and blood came down my ears and I squealed because of the snow.

Elizabeth Noble (9)
Walton Holymoorside Primary School, Chesterfield

An Unknown Figure

I opened the door. Trembling with fear as it creaked open. An unknown figure stepped into the light. My heart pounded as it stepped into my room.
'Do you want to go shopping?' it shouted.
'Mum, you gave me the shock of a lifetime!'

Matthew Poole (9)
Walton Holymoorside Primary School, Chesterfield

The Spooky Ride

I was on a spooky ride, when the train went through a tunnel. Googly, sticky bones pointed into the glass like pins. I screamed *'Argh! Argh! Argh!'*
When we were out of the spooky tunnel with pointy bones in the glass, the train was turning upside down. It was scary.

Emily Hall (9)
Walton Holymoorside Primary School, Chesterfield

Jurassic Park 3

We were on a plane and suddenly we crashed into a tree.
We were being chased by a Tyrannosaurus rex and got to a lab. Soon we were being chased by velociraptors. Someone had been taken by a velociraptor. We were trapped. We gave back the eggs.

Joshua Lunn (8)
Walton Holymoorside Primary School, Chesterfield

Images

The gargantuan wave lashed at the high walls of the galleon. Some drops of spray flew onto the starboard and flowed down past the tall mast. It collected in a haphazard puddle on the portside. A thin column of fork lightning struck the sail - a flaming beacon against the night.

Thomas Graus (9)
Walton Holymoorside Primary School, Chesterfield

The Fairy Folk

A boy called Artemis stole a fairy book and captured Holly Short. She was kept at a foul manor. The LEP stopped time and paid the ransom, then tried to kill him. He escaped with half the gold. The rest he had paid to Holly, so she would cure his mum.

Dominic Newman (9)
Walton Holymoorside Primary School, Chesterfield

306

The Fallen Tooth

I had a tooth, it was wobbling and I tied a string and tried to pull it out.
Later it didn't work, so I couldn't pull it out. I tried really hard but I couldn't.
Then on Friday, it was the morning, my tooth came out. I was really happy.

Reena Chomber (9)
Whitehall Primary School, Leicester

The Tooth Fairy

Katie's tooth fell out and she was thinking how strange that a small tooth fairy could pick up her pillow. She didn't sleep that night and saw her *tooth fairy!* They became friends, but the fairy had to go and they never, ever, ever saw each other again.

Ariane Patel (9)
Whitehall Primary School, Leicester

The Precious Stone

I had a gold stone which my beautiful mum
bought for me.
However, when I was going to school I lost
it. My mum was the best, she found it! Just
then we had a party and I named the stone
Faheema. Consequently me and my stone
became famous after all.

Faheema Shaikh (9)
Whitehall Primary School, Leicester

Discovery

I was walking down the street. I was a daredevil.
I was walking on the unknown. No one had
been there for thousands of years. I saw a
purple tail, it was a dinosaur! Consequently I
stopped to breathe for four seconds. I rubbed
my eyes and it was gone!

Gemma Sumaria (9)
Whitehall Primary School, Leicester

310

Feeling Seasick

I felt like I was going to drown. It was a blue colour. I was seasick, unhappy and frightened. Everyone could do it except me. It may have been morning but to me it was night. People were going to laugh. I knew it. I wish I could swim.

Muhammed Lambat (9)
Whitehall Primary School, Leicester

The Wardrobe

Ben had this wardrobe. He thought it was kind of scary. He thought there were monsters inside but there weren't. When he went to bed he always asked his mum to stay with him until he was asleep. But one night he realised there was nothing scary about the wardrobe.

Caprice Hill (9)
Whitehall Primary School, Leicester

Night At The Park

When I came back from school, the phone rang. It was my dad and he said, 'Meet me at the park at 7 o'clock.'
When I went it was pitch-black.
Suddenly, 'Surprise!' - It was my surprise party and I almost cried and it was the best day ever for me!

Milan Dayal (9)
Whitehall Primary School, Leicester

A Bizarre Experiment

One stormy night, the mad professor and his cat, Blacky, were trying to make a son. When he put all the stuff in the pot, it turned out as a terrifying monster. He said, 'Ello I am Garry!' The professor got a bucket of water and Garry melted down.

Eleanor Williams (8)
Whitehall Primary School, Leicester

Kerry And Her Dream

Kerry got into the car, they were going to the zoo. Dad started the engine - *broom, broom.* Kerry gradually fell asleep.
Kerry could not find her parents. Another person was driving *her* car. Was it a burglar or a thief? She screamed, her dream ended.
'What a dream,' she said.

Felicia Harrison (8)
Whitehall Primary School, Leicester

Walking Down The Street

It was night. I was walking down the street, it was unknown and deserted. Then, in front of me, I saw a big bright green face glowing like mad. It was a witch flying in the air with her black cat! I couldn't believe what I saw. I fainted!

Vanisha Solanki (8)
Whitehall Primary School, Leicester

316

Katie's Story

When Katie got home from school she heard some music. She got closer, she realised it was her house. She ran to her mum and dad. She burst into the door and they all shouted 'Surprise! Happy birthday.' All of her friends were there. Thank you everyone.

Chloé Adamson-Green (9)
Whitehall Primary School, Leicester

The Scary Ghost

One night a ghost came in my bedroom and put scary faces on the wall. It put videos in front of the door. I woke up, it was really cold. The window was already open and it pulled my quilt off me.

Kane Jenkins (9)
Whitehall Primary School, Leicester

The Stormy Evening

July 1999, it was a stormy night. I walked in my house, I saw a light beaming at me. A person came closer and closer, then took out a knife. I was sweating, he tried to stab me. So I dodged it, he dropped his knife then I grabbed him.

Alex Beric (9)
Whitehall Primary School, Leicester

A Hallowe'en Party

Saffiya and I were excited to see the fairy with golden hair at the Hallowe'en party. We felt very drab in our rags.
'You may have one wish!'
We tingled as the magic began to work. Our new costumes were excellent. We were excited and everyone had fun.

Aisha Seedat (9)
Whitehall Primary School, Leicester

322

Scared

The ball came to my feet. I was scared stiff.
What do I do? Do I pass it? Do I take it? Two of
the opposing team's monsters were charging
towards me. I had to decide quickly. My heart
was racing, I could hear my team yelling in the
background.

Abbie Measom (10)
Whitwick St John the Baptist CE Primary School, Coalville

The Budgie's Poem

It was coming to get me – the beast was so colossal, so bushy. I was coming out in a cold sweat. My heart was beating as fast as a cheetah's. I tried to fly away but no! I couldn't move an inch. It was coming, closer, closer, closer and closer.

Hannah Price (11)
Whitwick St John the Baptist CE Primary School, Coalville

Mad Scientist

It all started when a scientist tried to create a
new animal by mutating a snake and a spider,
but it went wrong. So I had to stop it but I was
too scared to move. Its brown legs and red
eyes and hairy legs scared me the most today.

James Gough (10)
Whitwick St John the Baptist CE Primary School, Coalville

325

The Race

Oh no, the time has come, it was my race! I felt
my heart was going to pop out of my mouth.
Five, four, three, two, one … the whistle blew.
Go!
I started to run. I quickly looked back, no one
behind me I was last! What to do now?

Isabel Wall (11)
Whitwick St John the Baptist CE Primary School, Coalville

326

A Surprise Fright

I lay there all alone, in the room, it was dark.
There was no noise at all, apart from that *bang
…*
bang … bang … tap … tap … tap … argh!
There it was … I can't say it …
A mother. It was time to get up. It was 6.30am in
the morning.

Shannon Walls (10)
Whitwick St John the Baptist CE Primary School, Coalville

The Room Of Doom

I was in a room. I heard footsteps. The footsteps got louder and louder every second. Suddenly a weird creature with a cloak came in. I shouted, 'What are you going to do with me?' but no answer. All I heard was purring. Suddenly the creature flicked back its head …

Jamie-Louise West (10)
Whitwick St John the Baptist CE Primary School, Coalville

328

The Fall

My hands shivered with fear, I was stranded on an old, high wall. I felt a breeze whip past me. I took a breath, then I fell forward. My heart was pounding madly. *Was this the end of my life?* I thought. As I fell, I hit the frozen ground.

Beth Fear (10)
Whitwick St John the Baptist CE Primary School, Coalville

Destruction

Five minutes to go … everyone out, the roof was cracking. I took no notice but now I lie here with monitors attached to me wherever I go! Was I – no it could not be possible – however much I tried, I could not sit up! Tell me what is happening …

Danielle Wykes (10)
Whitwick St John the Baptist CE Primary School, Coalville

330

The Potion

It was a dark, stormy night and Mum was out. I added an ingredient. A puff of smoke wafted up. The smell went up my nostrils and made me heave. Another ingredient went in, it exploded up into my eyeballs. The door opened. Mum said, 'Have you finished that cake?'

Isaac Street (11)
Whitwick St John the Baptist CE Primary School, Coalville

The House

'Where am I?' I shouted with fear. There were trees surrounding me as if I was trapped. I heard a voice whispering in my ear.
'Keep walking and go in the house!' said the voice.
I went in the house – *click* – the door slammed shut. *Argh!* I can't get out.

Kimberley Smallwood (11)
Whitwick St John the Baptist CE Primary School, Coalville

332

The Monster

The monster was here, I could sense it. My sword and shield had gone. All I had was my trusty pocket knife. What was that? I felt a quick jolt of pain. 'Oh no!' I screamed. I dropped the PS2 controller. I'd lost a life.

Jack Acton (11)
Whitwick St John the Baptist CE Primary School, Coalville

It's Getting Closer!

I can't bear it any longer. I have to run. I have this suspicion that I'm going to get killed at any moment. I suddenly heard the fierce growl of the Minotaur. *It's getting closer,* I thought. 'Ahh! Turn that movie off this instant,' said my mother.

Aaron Brotherhood (10)
Whitwick St John the Baptist CE Primary School, Coalville

The Haunted Mansion

There lay a black creature with bright red eyes.
It started walking up the stairs. *Bang! Bang!*
went the stairs, *creak!* went the door. It started
walking into my bedroom. It picked up my
favourite toy to get me.
'Lucy, it's time to wake up!'

Lauren Southwell (11)
Whitwick St John the Baptist CE Primary School, Coalville

The Cemetery

I was walking in the cemetery when suddenly dead people came out of the ground. I suddenly saw them making a circle around me. It started to run but I ran into a dead person. I started to shout, 'Dad! Dad!' then I heard my alarm clock.
Time for school.

Hannah Cross (10)
Whitwick St John the Baptist CE Primary School, Coalville

336

Torture

My brain was blanker than blank. Glancing at my watch, I broke out in a cold sweat, that trickled down my forehead. My hands were pale, sticky and shivery. As I stared forward, screaming in my head was the small sentence – 'Come on pencil, make words, the exam's almost finished!'

Claudia Esposito-Edge (11)
Whitwick St John the Baptist CE Primary School, Coalville

337

The Play

I stepped forward. A light shone in my eyes. Millions of faces stared at me. I gulped, I spoke a word but no sound came out. I broke out in a cold sweat. 'Thank you and I hope you enjoy the play,' I said at the top of my voice.

Tristan Skelding (10)
Whitwick St John the Baptist CE Primary School, Coalville

The Birthday Party

Sarah jumped up and down as she ran down the stairs. '*Wow!* This is the best birthday party ever,' Sarah shouted. She ripped all her presents open in seconds. All her family and friends came to her party. They had music, lots of food and they played lots of games.

Stacey Berridge (10)
Whitwick St John the Baptist CE Primary School, Coalville

Surprise Birthday Party

Bang! The door shut hard. Kelly tried turning
the door handle on the huge wooden door.
Kelly tried again and again and again. Seconds
later Kelly needed the toilet and after she tried
the handle again, the door opened.
'Happy birthday!' said Kelly's dad.
'Thank you everyone.'
'Happy birthday!'

Curtis May (10)
Whitwick St John the Baptist CE Primary School, Coalville

The Darkness

The darkness surrounded me. I stood deadly still, even though I was in my own house. I was scared. *Boom! What was that,* I thought to myself. I heard whispers.
'Surprise!'
'What's going on,' I asked.
Then I woke up. What a dream.

Lily Starkey (11)
Whitwick St John the Baptist CE Primary School, Coalville

341

The Gun

Bang! Bang! I ran. I'd been shot. *Oohh!* I'd lost a life. I dropped my PS2 controller. Someone shot me, I had lost a life.

Lauren Dennis (11)
Whitwick St John the Baptist CE Primary School, Coalville

342

Monster

Creak! The wooden door slowly swung open. A tall large figure stood in the doorway. Suddenly it stepped forward. Closer … closer … *'Boo!'* I screamed louder than a bell! Then I backed to the wall. It followed me. I crouched in a corner. 'Wuss!' it was my brother Damian.

Sarah Bonner (10)
Whitwick St John the Baptist CE Primary School, Coalville

The Water

There I was, leaning over the edge of a pool of torture, sour liquid tricking out of my mouth. I sat back up, the pain had stopped. Only for a moment though, suddenly there was a bump. The pain started again. I can't bear the sickness of a boat trip.

Billy Carroll (10)
Whitwick St John the Baptist CE Primary School, Coalville

344

The Creature Within The Egg

It lurks within the egg, splitting, cracking. The egg and creature dwell in the room of darkness with me! The egg is opened. The legs emerge, standing over its egg. The slimy creature appears. Leaping through the air. Gliding, its tail comes wrapping round my neck and … darkness, nothing more …

Jamie Croft (11)
Whitwick St John the Baptist CE Primary School, Coalville

345

The Vampires Of 45 And In

I was one of the last surviving humans, hiding in a den. I would have to go out sooner or later. I had to survive. I felt a burst of courage. I ran for my life, dodging the vampires left and right. I'm caught, I'm one of them – I'm on.

Kai Williams (9)
Whitwick St John the Baptist CE Primary School, Coalville

346

The Animal

I was in my room listening to the deadly footsteps creeping upstairs, when the wooden door swung open, smashing against the wall. I pulled the sheets over my head, dreading the animal coming in. it was time for my morning lick from my dog Jasper – gross!

Jack Brewin (10)
Whitwick St John the Baptist CE Primary School, Coalville

347

Arcade Doom

I inserted the coin, picked up the gun, green mouldy-looking zombies attacked. I shot but missed. The zombies go closer. I was out of bullets. They got closer and closer. Danger was at the end of my fingertips and suddenly an array of letters appeared – *'Game over!'*

Ashley Farmer (11)
Whitwick St John the Baptist CE Primary School, Coalville

348

Information

We hope you have enjoyed reading this book - and that you will continue to enjoy it in the coming years.

If you like reading and writing, drop us a line or give us a call and we'll send you a free information pack. Alternatively visit our website at www.youngwriters.co.uk

Write to:
Young Writers Information,
Remus House,
Coltsfoot Drive,
Peterborough,
PE2 9JX
Tel: (01733) 890066
Email: youngwriters@forwardpress.co.uk